PRINCESS THE CAT SAVES THE FARM

John Heaton

ISBN: 9781520675343

CHAPTER 1

"Clean your rooms!" the big woman person barks to the three children. "Make your bed. Vacuum. Clean the toilet."

Only the big man person has left my house for the day. The children usually leave the house for something they call "school." Something is different today.

My people clean like this when important people come to visit. I like it when they clean my house, my litter box, and Max's fur. Max's fur is mangy, and I don't like it mixing with my fur in my own territory. I don't like that my people fail to consult with me about potential guests. The guests never bring me gifts. Most people would come from distant lands to hear my wisdom.

I peer out from under the buffet in the kitchen to behold the chaos. Max has fun with this. Almost a fully-grown orange fluff-ball cat, his brain didn't grow with the rest of his body. He plays with any toy within reach. The children people think this is fun, but they eventually yell at him to stop messing up their organized piles. They are getting serious about cleaning the house; the big woman person even opens the attic.

The attic is the only place in my house where mice can hide from me. I still haven't managed to find my way up there, but I'm not too offended. My people hardly know how to get up there, either. The children sneak up there around Christmas time, but I can tell the big man person and the big woman person don't like going up there at all. But right before my all-seeing golden eyes, the big woman person hauls a ladder into my bedroom, removes a portion of the ceiling, and climbs into the attic.

"Wow," Max gasps in amazement, "did she just disappear?"

"Yes," I respond with an edge of sarcasm. "She disappeared, and I'm going to start driving cars, and I heard Patches came back from the dead."

"Really?"

"No, you goof," I say. "She went into the attic." Max walks cautiously over to the ladder, and he places his front paws on the second rung.

If people are coming to visit, I should warn Max. My people typically put me outside the whole time guests are here—a shocking breach of conduct.

My ears twitch and rotate slightly as I detect the rustling noises from the attic. I hear what sounds like the big woman person walking in the attic above me. Max jumps away in fear as things crash down out of the attic. Max comes to my side and snuggles up a little too close for my liking. One low growl, and Max moves away from me a few feet. I look at what has fallen out of the attic, and I remember these things. I usually only see them about once a year, and usually at the same time of year. They are suitcases.

If the big woman person is getting suitcases out of the attic, that must mean that people are leaving to somebody else's house. I never understand why my people want to leave me.

Chief has tried to explain it to me.

For a dog, Chief is rather wise—he has lived long enough. He once told me that some people have this disability in that they are "allergic" to cats. Apparently, some people are allergic to almost all animals. I'm not really sure how I feel about this. Simply labeling it as a medical condition is not a good excuse to let people off the hook from giving me the honor that I am due. I understand why some people would not feel worthy in my presence, but I also wonder why people tolerate such incredible flaws within their own population.

The big man person comes home as usual in the evening. He is a pretty sensible man, and he spends most of his days away from my home getting food for me and packing it into a can. The dry food is okay, but I love the canned food. He feeds me first, and once I'm done eating, I allow Max to eat. I decide against warning him about the impending changes.

It would only confuse him.

After dinner, the kid people play games, read books, and do homework. The oldest girl child spends the evening talking on the telephone. Tonight's conversation catches my attention.

"No, Friday night won't work," the oldest girl child says on the phone. "That's tomorrow night, right?"

My impeccable feline senses detect an affirmative from whoever is calling.

"No, me and my whole family are going on vacation," she says. "We're going to the country, actually. We are going to stay at Uncle Bill's farm!"

***

"*Awww*, Daddy, I'm going to miss Princess and Max so much," the youngest girl child says as she scoops me up in her arms the next morning.

I emit a low growl, and she drops me to the floor.

The young girl child has revealed her foolishness. She won't only miss me; she will falter along without purpose. "Who is going to take care of Princess and Max?" she asks. "Princess can take care of herself, but Max..."

Maybe she is not as foolish as I thought.

"Don't worry," the big man person says. "I'm going to pay somebody to take care of Max and Princess. They will make sure everything is okay. Besides, this might be the last time we can visit Uncle Bill—at his farm, anyways."

He will pay *somebody to come here?*

The big man person must realize that people should pay to see me. It is an honor to be in my presence, let alone feed me.

Out of mercy for Max, I need to find him so that I can warn him about what is in store for us. Perhaps I have developed a soft spot for him.

Max is not on top of the tropical fish tank. He's not on top of the TV. He's not under the buffet. Max isn't outside under the lilac bush or the apple tree, and I don't hear him yelling pitifully from the top of the willow tree. I hop up onto the back fence and walk the perimeter of my backyard. He's not going to the bathroom in the neighbor's yard. He is nowhere to be found. Maybe Chief has talked to Max or seen him recently.

"Hey, Chief," I say to Chief, who pretends to be asleep. "Do you know where Max is?"

"You don't know?" comes his lazy reply after a pause.

"Of course I do," I say, "but I need to keep you on your toes, make sure your canine instincts haven't faded."

Chief shakes his head in the negative.

Max is almost never in the front yard, but it is the last place to check. I quickly see he's not there, so I go in through the door on the side of the garage. I hop up onto the top of the large portable heaters—cars, as my people call them—and I see that Max isn't up there, either. He isn't playing with the string hanging down from the garage door opener. I can't find Max anywhere. I exit the cat door, into the front yard. As I wait for my people to let me back into my house, a boy approaches. He's younger than the oldest girl child, but older than the middle boy child. I recognize him immediately.

It's Todd.

I don't know if there's another person I dislike more than Todd. He is rebel scum. I scamper away and hide under the bush just as one of my people comes to open the front door for Todd.

***

Todd's toes protrude from the holes in his red sneakers as he walks by the bush I hide under. What must be fleas fall out of his dirty hair. I remember his hair to be pale blond and he always looks like he just got out of bed.

There is no way this beast will serve on my staff while my people are away on vacation. Todd doesn't know his place in society. He thinks he has the right to do whatever he wants with animals—even cats! The need to warn Max leaves my mind. I must find a way to persuade Todd to refuse to help my people while they are on vacation.

I dart out from under the bush away from the front door, through the cat door into the garage, and then I enter my eating room. I am alone with my and Max's food dishes, water bowls, litter box, and the large machines the people use to clean and heat their clothes. It's bizarre that people haven't figured out how to wash themselves like cats. Thank goodness I only need to lick myself.

Todd will be cleaning my litter box while my people are gone, and so I must make it as distasteful a task as possible. I can't stand doing this in my own house, but I need to for the greater good. I squat down beside the litter box, and I force myself to take a big poop. I scoot while doing the deed so that it streaks along the floor. Then I push Max's food bowl into it to grind it into the floor. Final touch: I scatter some litter onto the floor out of the box and spray it with pee. That should make cleanup horrific. I hurry out into my living room and hide under the couch.

The big man person and Todd are in the kitchen now. The big man person explains how they open the cans of my food so that they can give me my daily offering and tribute. Then they enter my eating room. I wait to hear Todd's response.

"That's unusual," the big man person says. "I will be sure to clean that up before we leave so that you don't have to worry about it. I don't think that has ever happened."

"Don't worry, sir," Todd says. "I will make sure to treat your cats right. They won't do these types of things. Everything will be just perfect when you get back."

Am I the only one who hears the plotting and deceit in his voice?

I dart out from under the couch and hop up onto the kitchen counter. I need a more aggressive tactic. I crouch behind the roll of paper towels. The big man person comes out of my eating room and leads Todd back to our kitchen, saying, "Let me show you those last few houseplants you need to water." The big man person walks by me without seeing me, but Todd spots me as he approaches. He narrows his eyes, and his grin exposes his crooked yellow buckteeth. It is as if he is saying, "I can't wait for this." I need to make sure that Todd never wants to see me again.

Once Todd's back is to me in the kitchen, I pull the same maneuver I typically use on dogs and coyotes: The Guillotine. I leap from the kitchen counter, sail through the air, and hook my front claws into Todd's shoulders. My fangs sink into the back of his neck while I scratch furiously with my rear claws. His neck is too thick for me to get ahold of, but I tear his shirt.

Todd yells, "What the—?!" and spins to get me off. Todd tears his shirt off in an effort to get rid of me. I hiss and yowl when I land on the ground.

I stare into Todd's eyes. Todd draws his foot back to kick me, but he restrains himself. His grin returns, and his yellow buckteeth stick out from his smile. He doesn't clean those yellow teeth nearly as often as he should. In response, I show my well cared for white fangs and release another hiss.

"Put some clothes on," the youngest girl child yells with laughter, seeing Todd shirtless and with red stripes on his back.

"See," the oldest girl child says, "I told you Princess can be mean." I'm not offended by this because I need help to persuade Todd he does not want to help my people while they are gone.

"That is definitely a first," the middle boy child wryly comments about my attack.

"That's yet another thing that has never happened before," the big man person says. "I expect the next ten days will be much less eventful. All you have to do is feed them. Princess will pretend you don't exist. If you witness any weird antics, it will probably be from Max. By the way, where is Max? Has anybody seen him?"

"Nope," all three kids say in unison.

Todd slips his shredded shirt back on, and the big man person leads him to the front door.

"Make sure you water those two plants in the living room, and we will be back in about ten days. If that changes, we will call your mom and dad."

"How much do you pay?" Todd asks.

"Two dollars a day," the big man person says. "Is that okay with you?"

"Of course."

The big man person takes a key out of his pocket and hands it to Todd. Todd accepts the key, and he walks out the front door.

"Don't worry about a thing," Todd says. "I will make sure everything, and especially your cats, are taken care of."

My efforts have failed. I wasn't able to dissuade Todd from assisting my people over the next ten days. For the first time in my life, I feel like peeing on my carpet. Perhaps it is time for me to move my kingdom to Canada. I can still feel the tingle from my old scars from a previous encounter with Todd. I haven't felt this sort of dread since the days of Snarl, that nasty coyote.

CHAPTER 2

I look out over my domain as I pace the perimeter of my yard from on top of the fence. Everything seems normal. The twin cats next door, Tweedledee and Tweedledum, play in their people's backyard. I suspect they found catnip. If they keep this racket up, they will scare my hunting game away. Or worse, they will attract coyotes or wolves.

"Hey, you two fur balls," I call out to them. "I don't care if you found catnip. Don't be so loud."

"What's the matter?" Tweedledee asks.

"Yeah," Tweedledum adds, "don't you want some catnip?"

"Never," I say. "I am always in full control of my faculties." I realize that's not something the twins would understand. "Stay in your people's yard, and don't even think about giving catnip to others."

"What did you think we were going to do?" Tweedledee asks.

"Drive a car to sell our catnip elsewhere?" Tweedledum chimes in. They both chuckle at themselves.

"We definitely are not sharing with Max, wherever he is," Tweedledee adds.

"You haven't seen him?" I ask.

They both shrug. Now is a good time to bring up an important topic.

"I have an opportunity for both of you to improve your position," I say. "I will stay in your house for the next ten days."

The white-furred twins glance askance at each other.

"Why?" Tweedledum asks slowly.

"Are your people rebelling?" Tweedledee asks.

Before I can correct their misconception, Tweedledum says, "Sorry, we will be driving a car all over the city selling catnip to other cats. We won't have time for a royal guest like you."

The twins snicker.

I don't have time for their insolence.

"Thanks for nothing," I say as I realize they have given me the solution to my problem. "Car" is what people call the large portable heaters they park in my garage to keep me warm. They will drive a car for vacation to visit Uncle Bill on his farm. The best way I can escape torment from Todd, who has not learned to respect cats, is to go with my people to their vacation.

The children seem excited about this vacation. How bad can it be? Perhaps the farm is really a resort. It's probably not quite up to the standards for a cat like me, but it will be better than Todd.

I make my way over to Chief's pen.

"Hey, Chief," I say to my trusted adviser. Chief doesn't respond. Chief is so old that he is afflicted by a people disease: arthritis. I'm worried that someday I will come to talk with Chief, and I will find that he, and all of his wisdom, has passed away.

"Chief!" I call out a little bit louder.

His eyebrows raise, but his head remains resting on the ground.

"My people are taking me to a resort," I say, shading the truth, "instead of hiring a juvenile who doesn't know how to treat cats properly while they are away on vacation, that is."

"You are taking Max with you, aren't you?" Chief asks. He still has not opened his eyes. I release a long sigh. Chief is right. I would love to go to a resort without Max, but I can't leave Max here with Todd.

"I will find Max, and let him know he's coming with me," I concede. Chief starts snoring, apparently satisfied by my response.

But if those twin fur balls had catnip, and Max was nowhere to be seen, where could Max be? Max loves catnip more than anything else. If the catnip didn't attract Max, I'm not sure how I'm going to find him.

I spend the rest of the night searching for Max, but I never find him. I begin to wonder if something serious happened to him. Did he sneak away? I decide that is unlikely. Nobody saw Max during the night, let alone see him leave my domain. My heart skips a beat as I consider the possibility that the coyotes are back in power. But again, nobody has spotted any coyotes.

When the sun is coming up, the big man person opens the garage. (I think he gave up trying to repair it.) Once he backs the car out onto the driveway, he opens the car doors to start packing. I sneak into the house through the garage. I hide under the buffet in the kitchen. Perhaps the people know something about Max that I don't.

"Where are the batteries for my music player?" the oldest girl child calls out to anybody willing to listen.

"Does my Carrot Patch doll get a seatbelt?" the youngest girl child asks the big woman person.

The middle boy child reads a book on the couch, pretending he doesn't hear or see anything. I peer out from under the buffet, and I see the big man person writing with a pen on some scraps of paper.

"Water the plants in the living room… Water the plants in the bedroom… Give the cats water every day… Give them one scoop of dry cat food, and one can of canned cat food every evening…" he mutters to himself as he writes.

"Where are Max and Princess?" the big woman person asks.

"We can't leave without saying good bye to Max and Princess," the youngest girl child says, clutching her doll to her chest.

"Yeah," the oldest girl child says. "We're not leaving until we find Max and Princess."

The big man person gives his response by reading out loud the note that he left for Todd to care for my house. After he reads, "Max and Princess are missing," he turns to the second page and continues. "If they do not return by tomorrow, call us at this phone number at Uncle Bill's farm."

"I'm sure Max and Princess will be fine," the big man person says. "They are resourceful cats, and they can take care of themselves better than you would expect. We're not going to delay our whole vacation just because our cats are acting weird. Todd will let us know if they don't come back by tomorrow, and then we can do something. But I guarantee that they will come back tomorrow, just like normal. We do not have to delay our vacation."

I sense the three children people are exchanging glances with each other, until the oldest girl child finally says, "Okay. But if Max and Princess aren't back by tomorrow, then we need to come home right away and call the police."

"And Animal Control, and the firefighters," the youngest girl child says.

"They probably just found some roadkill to eat somewhere," the middle boy child says. He shuts his book and gets up from the couch, as if it is such a burden to keep my couch warm.

"Everybody go to the bathroom one more time, and then get in the car," the big man person commands. Once everybody is out of the kitchen, I sneak out from under the buffet. I hop up onto the counter where the big man person left his note for Todd. I snatch the second page of the note in my mouth.

Before anybody sees me, I hop down from the counter, and I rush into my eating room. I dump the second page of the letter into my litter box, go to the bathroom on it (I'm just doing what the big man person said!), and I scratch some of the litter on top of the note. If I did this right, all Todd will know is that he is supposed to water some plants, and that Max and I are missing. He won't read the part about calling Uncle Bill because we are missing.

I exit my eating room into the garage.

"Max, are you here?" I ask one more time.

No response.

Well, I tried.

I rush out of the garage to the back of the car. I leap up into the car. I need to hide myself amongst the packed belongings in the car before the big man person comes to shut it. I see a perfect little niche between one of the rear wheel wells and a suitcase that doesn't perfectly fit. I plunge in to curl up before anybody sees me, but I land on something soft and furry.

It's Max!

***

"You found it, too?" Max stammers. He shakes nervously. "I promise I was going to come tell you about this place. I found it yesterday when the big man person was putting stuff into the car. Curious, I hopped in, and this place was so cozy… And I wondered what a large portable heater would be like on the inside. I couldn't resist this spot, and I've stayed here."

"I'm sure you would've told me about this wonderful sleeping spot eventually," I say.

"Of course, of course," Max says with relief. "Why are you here? Never mind, I need to get some food and go to the bathroom."

"Don't go," I say.

"*Umm*, okay," Max says. "I could go pee in here, but that would ruin this napping spot until our people clean it."

"No," I say, "you need to hold it."

"What?" Max says.

"*Shhhh,*" I whisper to Max. "Stay absolutely quiet. I will explain later. Trust me."

The car doors open, and my people pile into the car. The big man person has not joined us yet. He must be locking all the doors to my house.

"Why do I always have to sit in the middle?" the middle boy child says. Nobody answers. I hear music faintly playing. It must be from the big girl child's headphones. People really do have horrible hearing. They even need to stick their music directly in their ears.

The youngest girl child makes baby talk with her doll. Max is about to get up and go play with her. I push him down with my front paw and give him a glare. He gets the message, but he grimaces at me. He really does need to go to the bathroom.

A few minutes later, the big man person gets into the car. The car starts, and we begin moving. The only experience I've ever had like this is when the people take me to the vet in the car. I went there after my victory over the coyotes, and I went there to get "fixed" earlier in life. I didn't miss Patches after that visit to the vet.

We drive for what feels like a long time. I clamp one of my paws over Max's mouth for quiet.

The youngest girl child plays with her doll, the middle boy child grumbles and complains, and the oldest girl child blares music in her headphones. Classic pop music plays quietly on the AM radio, and the big man and woman people talk with each other.

Suddenly, the youngest girl child calls out, "I've got to go pee! I've got to go pee!"

"Uugh," the big man person groans.

"Already?" the big woman person says. "We left not even half an hour ago."

"I gotta go. I gotta go."

"Fine," the big man person says. "Hold it until the next gas station."

The youngest girl child continues to mumble, *"I gotta go, gotta go."* Max clenches his teeth to hold his pee, too. I'm not sure he can hold it long enough. He looks sick to me.

I feel the car slow, turn, and then stop. The doors open, everybody gets out, and I look at Max. His fur doesn't seem quite right, even for Max's long, orange and white fur. His eyes are an odd shade of green. I don't mean the shade of green they should be. They are sickly green.

"I'm going to be sick," Max says, "and I've really, really, got to go to the bathroom."

The big man person opens the back of the car, and Max pukes on the nearest suitcase.

"Max?!" the big man person yells when he sees both Max and half-digested cat food dripping from his luggage.

Max leaps out and runs past him.

"Max?! Get back—" the big man person says as he turns to see Max, who is now watering a nearby bush. He picks Max up, tosses him in the car, and shuts the door. I look out the window as the big man person jogs into the gas station.

"Is there anything to eat?" Max asks.

I ignore him.

"We can't go back home," I say. "You don't want to know what's back at my house."

"Of course we're going to go back to our house," Max says.

"You don't get it, do you?" I say. "Our people are going on vacation. They are not going back to my house for another ten days."

"Oh, that kind of hurts my feelings," Max says. "Why would they want to be without us for so long?"

"I can't imagine," I say with an edge of sarcasm. "There is nothing good for us at my house. There is only Todd."

"What is a 'Todd?'" Max asks.

"You don't want to know," I say as the big man person jogs out of the building with a roll of paper towels. He opens the back of it and starts cleaning up Max's puke.

"Princess is here too?" he says when he sees me. "Why not?"

"You're welcome, Max, for my people cleaning up your mess," I tell Max. The woman person and the three children return from the gas station.

"Max!" the youngest girl child calls out.

"Hey, Max," the oldest girl child says. The middle boy child doesn't say anything, but he doesn't frown.

"Are Max and Princess going to go with us on vacation?" the youngest girl child asks.

"Yuck," the big man person says as he wipes up the last spot of Max's puke and throws the paper towel into the garbage. "I don't want to turn back. By the time we got back home, drop the cats off at our house, and get back to here, it would be almost an hour."

"I can't wait anymore for this vacation," the big woman person says.

"Me neither," the big man person says, "and Uncle Bill could use some cats for a little bit, anyways. I don't think he has cats anymore. It could be their last chance to experience the farm."

Not a single cat is willing to take Uncle Bill in as their person?

The cats are gone, but Uncle Bill is still there. This perplexes me, but I decide to nap instead of mulling it over in my mind.

My car tumbles down the highway. I decide to stay in my sleeping spot, but Max rides in the middle part of the car with the children. It's louder now as the kids play with Max. The big man person and the big woman person put things in their ears to prevent them from hearing the noise. They already hear poorly enough; they must be completely deaf now. Even the middle boy child lets a smile slip from having me and Max in the car. Max purrs, and I guess he's getting his tummy rubbed.

Nobody touches my tummy, I think to myself as I doze off to sleep and dream of my long lost crush, Patches.

CHAPTER 3

"We're here!" the big man person booms.

The car doors open, and my people get out of the car.

"Uncle Bill! Aunt Susie!" the big man person says.

Uncle Bill and his wife must have been waiting for me.

"Great to see you," says a kind baritone voice that must be Uncle Bill.

"Welcome," Aunt Susie says.

"How was the drive?" Uncle Bill asks.

"Especially with three kids in the car?" says Aunt Susie.

"The kids were great," the big man person says, "but we are late because of our cats."

"How's that?" Uncle Bill asks.

"I hope you don't mind a few extra furry guests while we're here," the big man person says. He opens the back of the car. Max hides as I stand on the edge of the back of the car, careful not to touch remnants of Max's puke.

Uncle Bill is tall, bald, and heavyset. Aunt Susie is much shorter, with gray hair.

"Wonderful," says Uncle Bill, "we could use some cats. I don't know what happened to ours..."

The people continue talking as I inspect the smells of the farm. I recognize the odor of green grass, but there are other smells from plants and and animals that I'm not familiar with. My nose confirms what Uncle Bill said: there are no other cats. However, I do smell a dog.

And then, I hear a dog.

A dog cautiously creeps up to the back of the car. He is not much bigger than me, but he has an elongated body with a dark coat. He growls and bares his teeth. Max remains hidden in the car, but I don't flinch.

"I am Princess, the Empress of Rover Boulevard of the White Rock, and Slayer of the wicked coyote, Snarl." Instead of assuming a posture of homage, the dog gives a confused look, but then he resumes growling. I guess I should not expect country dogs to understand how important I am.

"You must pay me my due as your superior," I say. "If you don't treat me properly as your royal guest, this farm will never be an honored resort. Trust me. You don't want to be on my bad side."

"Don't you know who I am?" the small dog counters, trying to sound tough. "I'm the guard of this ranch."

"But you appear to be a miniature dog," I say. "We are about the same size. You are shaped like a hotdog. You must be a wiener dog."

"I am a dachshund," he says with a pause between each word. "I am of a noble breed from—"

"From where? The sausage factory?"

"No."

I sense he is searching for an insult to use against me, but he can't find one.

"My name is Benny, and I'm the guard dog on this farm."

"What happened to the cats?"

"There hasn't been a cat for a few months," Benny says.

"So I will have to assume rule for the next week or so." *Does my work ever end?* "You can be of service, Benny. Your first task is to introduce me to everybody as their temporary ruler."

I expect Benny to give initial resistance, which I will have to overcome, but Benny doesn't respond. Benny's gaze is elsewhere. His eyes are wide open as he looks towards Uncle Bill's house. A small white dog walks along the porch of Uncle Bill's farmhouse. Instead of being shaped like a hotdog, this dog has fluffy and curly fur. I believe this would be called a poodle.

The small white poodle runs towards Aunt Susie near my car, yapping along the way, and Aunt Susie picks her up. I grin to myself. Benny has revealed his weakness so easily. He is in love with this little white poodle.

"I will give you cats a spot in the barn for now," Benny pronounces with a loud voice. I know he's trying to impress the poodle. "Tonight there will be a weenie and marshmallow roast."

Max sticks his head out from hiding.

"They're going to cook you at the weenie roast tonight?" Max says.

"No!" Benny responds.

"Take me to my accommodations," I tell Benny. "I'm sure I have been upgraded to the penthouse suite? And, by the way, that is Max. I apologize."

Benny doesn't say anything as he walks towards the barn.

Max and I follow him, and I decide this is a good time to use my leverage on Benny.

"Who is that nice white dog?" I ask Benny. "She seems like an uncommonly good dog."

"Her name is Pearl," Benny says, "and she's my… my friend."

"Really?" I say. "You want her to be your girlfriend, don't you?"

"She's not my girlfriend yet," Benny says, "but she will be. You wait and see."

"I'm sure I could assist you," I tell Benny. "Us girls stick together, and if you serve me well, I could say something to her about you."

As we reach the barn's large front entry doors, I see a smaller fenced-in area attached to the barn. I also notice a tractor near a scarecrow in the distance.

Before we go in, I say to Benny, "Think about it, Benny. If you prove yourself a good subject to me, you will win the girl. You don't want to end up like someone who doesn't serve me well, do you?"

Benny thinks it over.

I suspect that the idea of having Pearl as his girlfriend will make him do nearly anything.

***

As we pass the fenced area attached to the barn, I smell an animal I have never smelled. I jump up onto the top of the fence, half expecting to see Chief in the pen, waiting to give me advice. Instead, I see a bunch of mud. But I do see a magical animal that I have only heard of. Not a unicorn, but a pig—that wonderful source of pork chops, bacon, pork loin, and many other delectable goods. I'm shocked when the pig talks to Benny.

"Who are the new kids, Benny?" the pig asks.

I can't allow an answer that would imply I'm a "kid."

"I am Princess, Empress of Rover Boulevard of the White Rock, Slayer of the wicked coyote Snarl." Instead of bowing in awe, the pig stands on his hind legs to peek through the fence at Max. He is behind me, rolling in the grass. Max bats a dandelion up and down, up and down. Although he is full grown, he still acts like a kitten.

"Is that your court jester?" the pig asks. "He's obviously not a guard or soldier."

"His name is Max," Benny jumps in. "And he too, apparently, is a cat."

"I admit," I say, "that Max is a bit of an embarrassment, and inexcusable at times." It's best to be upfront about shortcomings and faults. They can help build trust for the future. Now that I think about it, I wonder if Max could stay on the farm here. Or perhaps he could get lost in the nearby forest. Definitely an idea to think about.

"Are you in charge, or is little Benny in charge?"

"My name is Elmer," the pig says, "and you should know better than anybody that dogs are not born to lead. They are born to follow. So obviously, then, he follows and does what I say."

"How has this farm not plunged into anarchy and chaos?" I ask. "There are no cats here."

"I've been around long enough to know that there are many places where there are no cats," Elmer replies. "And I'm not worried, to say the least, that there are no longer any cats here. However..."

I look back to see that Max has found yet another dandelion to unleash his ferocity upon.

"You and Max," Elmer continues, "could be useful to rid this farm of vermin. Come on in, and I will show you your stall."

"We have just met," I say, "and you are a pig, and so I will forgive this oversight of yours, but I should not have to point out that, again, I am Princess." I pause for a few seconds so that it sinks in, but it doesn't seem to change Elmer's reaction. "I don't stay in the animal quarters. The people are not going to eat me, after all. I stay in houses, and I allow my people to serve me by canning my food, dishing it out, warming my beds for me, and other such tasks that give them purpose in life."

Elmer and Benny exchange glances. I suspect this is all news to Elmer.

It's time I go on the offensive now that I have caught him off guard.

"Why didn't they eat you, pork chop?" I ask.

"Some of us," Elmer says, "transcend our role in society and do more than simply fulfill social norms."

"Like that yapping footstool, Pearl?" I ask.

"All the animals on this farm stay in or near the barn, except for one: Pearl. She rarely comes out."

So, I will need to find a way to get Pearl out of the house, or Benny into the house.

"Since you are new to this," I say, "and our visit was unexpected, I will temporarily overlook your oversight, but let me explain to Max. He is a bit simple, and it may take some clarification."

I hop down from the fence and go to Max as he thrashes a third dandelion.

"For a short time," I tell Max, "we will stay in that filthy barn. But our suffering will have a purpose. We will do reconnaissance so that we can take over the farm and make this a colony that pays tribute. If we are patient, we can exert our authority with only minimum bloodshed."

"Okay," Max says as he spits yellow petals from his mouth.

"Come on."

Max follows me back to Elmer's pen.

"I will introduce you to everybody," Elmer says.

Just as Elmer pushes the barn door open, a loud crash from the side of the barn makes us jump. Elmer rushes to the side. We all follow. A side barn door gapes open, and animals gush out. Bleating, neighing, and all other sorts of ridiculous noises fill the air.

I roll my eyes and sigh.

This is what happens when there's no cat around to keep things in order.

More astonishingly, as soon as I'm done rolling my eyes, I see Elmer chase the farm animals, attempting to herd them back into the barn.

What kind of farm does Uncle Bill run?

***

I watch with amusement as what seems like Noah's Ark has been dumped out into the grassy field. I exaggerate. It's not Noah's Ark. It's really just a lot of animals that probably wouldn't have made it on to Noah's Ark. Max is also mixed up in the chaos. I can't blame him, though. Just like people, he is simply doing what everybody around him is doing.

Speaking of people, Uncle Bill notices the ruckus, and he comes running, waving his arms and yelling at the animals. I think he uses some words my big people don't allow. Aunt Susie clutches Pearl, whose eyes are as big as my food bowl. She's witnessing what can happen if the bourgeoisie and proletariat get riled up.

Elmer runs as fast as his stubby legs can carry him as he attempts to herd the animals back into the barn. He's not doing half bad; for a pig, that is. Benny trots along the perimeter of the fence, growling and barking. He glances at Pearl to see if she notices his "heroics." I take stock of all the animals I see: two sheep, two goats, and a big cow are the first ones I notice. I also see the horse Max was trying to keep pace with.

I shake my head and laugh to myself. I'm not sure if I've ever laughed this hard.

This is what happens without a cat.

Elmer the pig and Uncle Bill eventually herd all the animals back towards the entrance of the barn, but I hear the animals complaining.

"You let us down..."

"It's your fault..."

"This shouldn't have happened..."

"You said you could protect us..."

This has my attention.

I sense a vacuum of power, and I know they will need me to step in. However, I'm not sure I want to step into this mess. It could be like stepping into a pile of dog poop.

Once all of the animals are back in the barn, Uncle Bill inspects everything, muttering more of those forbidden words.

"Eggs are missing from the chicken coop," Uncle Bill reports to Aunt Susie. There must be a chicken coop attached to the barn on the other side that I have not seen. Uncle Bill walks away, shaking his head and muttering.

All the animals mutter, too. All of their eyes are as wide as my food bowl, but from fear, not surprise.

"You let your guard down because of those two new city-slicker cats," I hear from one of the animals. Other animals nod in agreement and voice similar things.

"Do you guys have coyotes?" Max asks the animals. "You should know that we have already slain the mighty coyote, Snarl. Have you heard the story?"

"Don't embarrass yourself, Max," I say to him. "If coyotes were the problem, they would have taken more than just eggs."

"Since you're new here," Elmer says to me, "it's only fair you know there are some problems brewing. Something, or somebody, or somebodies, have been trying to take over this farm. They use fear, and we've all felt the threat growing since Alfie left."

"Alfie?" I ask, even though I know the answer to my own question just as I ask it.

"Alfie was the cat who used to be here," Elmer says. He's reluctant to admit things were better when a cat was in charge.

"I'm sorry this happened," Benny says to Elmer, "and I accept responsibility that it may have happened because we let our guard down because of our new guests. I promise to increase guard activities. I will double my patrols, and I will make sure this doesn't happen again."

For the first time, the horse speaks up.

"Everybody is dying to know, Benny," the horse says. "How did you feel when you first heard that the Phantom struck again."

"The 'Phantom' is what you're calling it?" Benny asks.

"Everybody is dying to know the real story," the horse continues, "and they want to hear from your perspective, the guard dog."

Benny starts to answer, but I can hardly listen from my astonishment. The talking horse seems like he's one of those people on my big man person's television who interviews people. I think he's called a newsman, or an anchor. When I'm able to focus again on what he's saying, he is interviewing the cow, apparently named Daisy. (What a lack of originality.)

"Well, Ned, this sort of volatility in the farm would lower tourist demand," Daisy says, "and potentially the demand for commodities like dairy, wheat, and corn. If this invisible threat could be countered, that would do a lot to help investor confidence. For now, this could be a great time to buy if you feel like this threat is temporary. If you are not confident of that, it is time for you to sell."

I have no idea what this cow is talking about.

Ned has moved on to the next animal to interview. Elmer comes over to me and talks to me on the side.

"Alfie, the old cat who used to be here," Elmer says, "taught us that we should achieve our dreams. He said that we could become whatever we wanted. I always wanted to be a sheepdog. I just dream of bringing in the herd and driving the cattle. I heard stories about it when I was a piglet, and I think I even remember seeing a movie about it. People told me that I was just gonna be somebody else's breakfast someday. But no, I wanted to be a sheepdog. Alfie taught us that we could be whatever we dreamed. I dreamed I would be a sheepdog, and so that's what I've been doing."

I need to learn more about Alfie.

"Benny," Elmer continues, "dreams of being a guard dog. He thinks he can be on a K-9 unit for the police someday." I resist pointing out that he's really just a wiener dog. "I think you already noticed that Ned dreams of being a talk show host. He wants to talk to the stars of the world. Over there," Elmer says as he nods towards the two sheep, "are Gus and Betsy. They love art, and they fancy themselves to be art critics."

I focus in on Gus and Betsy's discussion.

"It is about time that the Monet exhibit comes to the Art Institute," Gus says. "I could simply spend all day at the Art Institute gazing at those Monet paintings. His brush strokes are simply brilliant."

"I wish we had water lilies like that here on our farm," Betsy replies dreamily.

Elmer continues his explanation about the animals.

"Daisy," Elmer says, "wants to be a financial investor. And Alfie, well, he's been gone for a while, but he really was our mentor. He even got David and Lisa to discover what they want to be."

After a pause, Elmer asks everybody, "Where is David?"

He looks around the barn frantically. I follow Elmer to a goat.

"Where's David?" Elmer asks the female goat.

"He wanted to go foraging for some organic mushrooms," she says.

"David didn't want to go into the forest to forage, did he?" Elmer asks.

"David does not trust the trash Uncle Bill feeds us. Just because we're goats does not mean we can't be vegan."

"Vegan means they only eat organic plant food," Elmer whispers to me.

Then I hear a new voice.

"Yes." The voice comes from above me. "That trash is so commonplace. Can you imagine? Instead of caviar, I don't even get quail eggs!" I look up to see a rat.

"That," says Elmer to me quietly, "is Wyatt, the rat. He fancies himself to be a millionaire."

This is an excellent chance for me to exert my rule and authority. All Max and I need to do is go out and find David in the woods. Having done that, I will prove that I am the most successful leader here. I will not have to use force to take over this farm.

"I'm sure Max and I can recover David easily," I tell Elmer as I start to walk out. Benny has heard what I said, and he runs up to follow me out the barn.

"There are serious security risks, ma'am," Benny says.

"Let them go on their own," Elmer says. Benny stops following, apparently torn between helping me and listening to Elmer.

"So, where are we going?" Max says as we exit the barn. "What are we doing?"

We enter the field, pass the tractor and the scarecrow, and then we leap the fence. I can't imagine what is unsafe about the forest ahead of us. As I approach the forest, I sense Elmer is hoping we will disappear.

"Be careful in that forest!" Elmer calls out to us from the barn.

How hard can it be to find a vegan goat?

CHAPTER 4

Max and I enter the woods, officially leaving Uncle Bill's farm. The trees aren't dense at first, and I can still see the tractor and scarecrow. However, after another minute, the trees are close together, and the canopy crowds out sunlight. I always imagine that forests are full of life, but this forest feels too dark to sustain much life. There is almost no noise from birds in the branches or vermin on the ground. An occasional slight breeze is all that makes movement or noise.

"Where are we go—" Max starts before he changes mid-word. "Gross! Something got me! It's a horrible beast!" Max calls out as he struggles to free himself from an invisible captor.

"Hold still," I command. "It's a common spiderweb."

"A giant spider is going to eat me?" Max says with terror.

"No," I respond. "Relax. Stop moving and walk away. See? It surprised you, but it's only a simple spiderweb."

"I guess we've lost the element of surprise," Max says sheepishly.

"Yes," I say, "but you found something else." The spiderweb in shreds was attached to a berry bush that has been picked clean.

"Do you see goat tracks near you?"

Max looks around.

"*Umm,*" Max says, "I honestly have no idea what goat tracks look like." Maybe I'm getting soft on Max, but I pass up the opportunity to mock him and instead admit that I don't really know either.

"I think we can assume our vegan goat David has been here," I say. "Let's follow the trail."

Max follows me as I pad my way stealthily through the forest, following the trail of barren berry bushes. Hoof prints lead from one bush to the next. I'm still amazed at how lifeless the forest feels. I have a bad feeling we are in a trap, or somebody is watching us. Perhaps both.

The trail leads us into a dense thicket that sinks into a small ravine. A creek runs through it.

"I'll bet David is down there," Max says, "but those bushes look real thorny."

"Wait here," I tell Max. "I'm going to climb this tree and look around."

"Okay," Max says, "well, I'll make sure that, well I don't know, I'll..."

"Don't follow a butterfly off somewhere," I say as I ascend the tree.

From my perch I see into the thicket below, and into the ravine. A goat stands in the middle of it, munching on berries amid the thorns, apparently oblivious to the fact that he's so far from home.

My eyes follow the creek up the ravine, and I spot something that makes the fur on my back stand on edge. If I didn't know better, I would say that Todd and three members of his gang are sitting and playing a card game. It can't be Todd, but they are definitely of the same species as Todd: dirty and mischievous, delighting in trouble. They have some food and drinks, and their bicycles lay nearby.

There are five bicycles, but only four boys.

A loud crack splits the air in the tree behind me.

"Hey, guys!" a fifth teenage boy yells out to his friends playing cards, "I've found some more. Let's get them!"

I dash down as the boy raises one hand towards me and pulls back the other to take aim. A projectile whistles by my head as Max turns to follow me as I run by. I plunge into the thicket where David is munching on his next berry bush.

"Help!" Max calls out behind me. "Princess!" I turn back, and I see Max's horribly long fur tangled in the brambles. He can't move. I go back to the edge of the thicket and try to pull him in, but his squirming only entangles him more. I turn to face the boy who approaches the thicket. His four friends crash through the forest towards us.

I puff fur, bare my fangs, and wait for the boy to get closer so I can pounce. He stops well outside of my leaping range and gives a chuckle. I see him grab a shiny metal ball from his pocket, place it into something attached to a rubber hose, and pull it back.

A slingshot.

He's missed twice, but I know it's only a matter of time before he hits me or Max.

I must rush at him, but I'm no match for five boys who have the idiocy of dogs but the confidence of cats.

"Don't leave me!" Max calls out.

I can't do anything to help Max.

At least I could survive and maybe get away with David if I leave Max now. I will have to leave Max behind.

Before I can do anything else, another voice rings out in the forest, shocking both me and the boys.

YOWWWL!

A giant roar freezes even the cocky boys. I've never heard one of my distant relatives. It must be one of the big cats, a mountain lion.

"Let's get out of here!" the boys yell as they turn and run back to their bikes. Max is nearly free of the thorns, but he won't know which direction to flee. I dare not get any closer. I'm afraid that if I help, I'll only get caught in the thorns myself.

***

The roar of the mountain lion not only scares me, Max, and the teenage boys, but it also frightens David out of his eating stupor. He's large enough to pound out of the thicket without being caught. As he passes, one of his horns dislodges Max. Max and I run alongside David towards the farm. The trees thin out, and we reach the fence. Max and I rush under the middle bar, but David leaps over the top of the fence. As we race past the tractor and scarecrow to the barn, I am impressed that David outpaces me.

The three of us storm into the barn, and all heads turn towards us. Lisa, David's wife, shouts with glee.

"David! David! You made it back!"

The other animals give signs of joy and approval, whether it be clapping of hooves, wagging of tales, or neighs and grunts of happiness. This is my time to take credit for the good that I have done. This is the easiest way to assert my power. I show my subjects that I am able to benefit them, and they will willingly put themselves under my control. Once they are addicted to me doing things that they are unable or unwilling to do for themselves, they will gladly accept my authority over them.

"Loyal members of Uncle Bill's farm," I call out to the animals in the barn as I hop up onto a barrel. "I promised I would find this wayward goat and bring him back home safely to his wife and friends." I look out over the animals in the barn, but they are not as excited as I expect them to be. Ned, the interviewing horse, speaks up first.

"Is that how it really happened, David? Did this simple gray tabby house cat rescue you from the cruel clutches of the dark forest? The forest into which even Alfie entered and never returned? And from which some mysterious evil slowly creeps into our farm?"

I imagine Ned handing the microphone over to David, or sticking it in his mouth. David answers.

"We were all going to die, except for the mountain lion, that is," David begins. "I had never heard such a ferocious roar until I heard that roar from the mountain lion in the forest."

"What led you into that treacherous forest?" Ned asks.

"I noticed some excellent looking berries while seeking mushrooms. Surely they are full of antioxidants, but they were just beyond the fence," David explains. "Since they were outside the farm, I figured they were likely wild and organic. I hopped the fence and made my way over to the berry bush. It was a mix of red berries, raspberries, blackberries, and an assortment of other fine berries. They had fewer chemicals than what I am accustomed to on the farm. I followed a trail of berry bushes deeper and deeper into the forest, intoxicated by these delightful berries."

Ned continues interviewing David, but I notice that David's account differs significantly from reality.

"The mountain lion was stuck in the thicket," David tells Ned and his enraptured audience. "He eagerly hunted me, seeking my succulent meat for his own feast. But when he got stuck in the thicket, he yelled out in pain."

Of course, I know it was really Max who was caught in the thicket. None of us ever actually saw the mountain lion.

"At the sound of his ferocious roar," David says, "I bolted out of the thicket, and I gave him a fierce kick in the face with my hoof. Then, as I raced towards this farm, these two traitorous cats, who are certainly allied with the mountain lion, continued to chase me back to the farm. And here they are, in our very own barn."

Now all the animals stare at me with a mix of wonder and anger. Benny growls.

"Those two new cats," David says with a hoof pointed at me, "who just arrived are on the same side as the mountain lion. They led the mountain lion to me in the forest. Why else would they so boldly enter the dark forest?"

Certainly not for organic berries or mushrooms—antioxidants or whatnot.

"Traitors!" David yells out.

Before I set the record straight, Elmer speaks up.

"The story is incomplete," Elmer calls out. "We do not carry out justice by mob rule. May I remind all of you that Princess and Max are guests of Uncle Bill? Remember: if the mountain lion were our true enemy, he wouldn't steal just chicken eggs. Coyotes would have eaten the chickens, and a mountain lion would have eaten the chickens, and probably some of us, as well." There are murmurs from the crowd, some of them in agreement, and some of them expressing disapproval. I roll my eyes over the foolishness of these simple animals.

"Don't forget the weenie roast this evening," Elmer says. "The people will all sit around the campfire, sing songs, and cook hot dogs over a fire. Then they will roast marshmallows. Without further proof, treat Princess and Max as Uncle Bill's guests.

"The weenie-roast will be a fun time for all of us, and it should give us all something to distract us from the troubles at hand. I don't think I need to remind all of you that under no circumstances should any of us go near the forest. Stay away from the fence. If David can hop the fence, then a mountain lion could leap over it with ease."

As the animals resume their normal affairs, Elmer approaches me.

"You're innocent until proven guilty," Elmer says, "but you had better not do anything suspicious."

I think that's a warning. I'm stunned by the lack of gratitude for saving David.

***

The weenie roast is quite the major event. All of the animals are let out of the barn in the evening to freely roam the grazing area. Ned the horse pulls a cart full of hay, and the kids ride in the back of it. It's called the hay bale ride. Uncle Bill even gets a rope and tries to have the kids take some lasso practice on some of the animals. David and Lisa don't think this is very exciting at all since they are the main targets.

"The practice of lassoing animals is a holdover from a more barbaric time when people used it to capture and kill animals for food," David informs everybody.

The three children take joy in chasing Elmer as he tries to herd the animals. Even the middle boy child is having fun.

The main event, of course, is the large fire that Uncle Bill starts. A roaring fire, encircled by small stones, reaches several feet up into the sky. The children love grabbing sticks, logs of wood, anything that can burn, and throwing them into the fire. Their parents don't love this so much. Max and I, along with several other animals, curl up several feet away from the fire. It's kind of like a sunbeam. In just the right spot, it's not too hot, but it is cozy warm. The boy child sits mesmerized by the flames, probably concocting a plan to burn something, and I sidle up to his leg. Max sprawls luxuriously across both the girls' laps with his tummy in the air. The heat from the fire warms his tummy, and the girls rub it. Benny paces the perimeter to keep guard.

The fire dies down once the kids stop adding fuel. Uncle Bill cooks up some hot dogs and baked beans over the fire. Even us animals get some. The people love this event, and even I am starting to enjoy it. Once we've stuffed our faces full, Uncle Bill says it's time to tell campfire stories.

"All of you just arrived," Uncle Bill says to my people, "but if you explore around here, you will find lots of interesting things. Nobody lives at the farm next door. The house and barn are empty since a mean developer has been trying to force us farmers off our land so he can build condominiums. I'm the only one left around here, but there is a another barn in the forest. That barn has been deserted for years, but for a different reason. Some people say it's not completely empty." I look at the other people, and they stare at Uncle Bill, desperate to hear more about this barn. "It's not empty at all. Rather, it's haunted."

"Now, Uncle Bill," the big man person says, "don't make this too scary. I want the kids to sleep well tonight."

"Oh, these kids are plenty old," Uncle Bill says.

"Yeah, we're old enough," all three children people say in unison.

"Your kids will love the story," Aunt Susie says. I notice she's not holding Pearl. Pearl is the only animal not here.

"Of course, there's a story behind the haunted barn," Uncle Bill says. "Your Great-Grandpa Rasmussen used to live in these here woods in a house. He also built a barn. But one winter was particularly hard. It was the hardest winter they had ever faced. Remember, they didn't have electricity and heaters like we have today. Food became scarce. What's worse is that a mountain lion came and ate all the livestock."

At the mention of the mountain lion, I and all the other animals perk up.

"Great-Grandpa Rasmussen knew he would have to go hunting in the dead of winter in snow to find food. He also knew he had to kill that mountain lion. Otherwise, the mountain lion would take all the food for himself. Well, it turns out another huge storm hit while he was hunting, and Great-Grandpa Rasmussen was never seen again. Nobody ever found his body. Folks say the ghost of the mountain lion will never allow anybody else to rule the forest."

I look at the children's faces. Burning coals reflect in their eyes as they listen in wonder.

"Great-Grandma moved away with the kids, and the house was eventually torn down. The family still owned this land, but nobody lived here for a long time. The land passed to the next generation, until it came to me, your dear old Uncle Bill. Now I've built a nice house for myself and your Aunt Susie here, but the old barn from Rasmussen still stands. Some people say these woods and the old barn are haunted by that mountain lion. Some people swear that you can even hear that mountain lion releasing his ferocious yowls in the woods, even today."

I look at all the other animals. All their eyes are wide open, as if they are looking at a double feeding in their food trough. Even Benny has stopped pacing like a guard dog.

"So," Uncle Bill continues, "I don't think any of you should be going near that old barn. You can find it in the woods easy enough, but don't go near it, and don't go inside it."

Everybody sits silently for several minutes as the coals glow until the big man person finally says, "Anybody know any *funny* campfire stories?"

A few seconds later, thankfully, Aunt Susie fills the silence. She tells some goofy stories about the old animals and what they used to do. Instead of listening, us animals ponder the mountain lion and the haunted barn. I look over and notice Max has moved off the girls' laps. He cuddles with Benny.

Some guard dog.

After a few more stories from Aunt Susie, the youngest girl child falls asleep, and the eyes sag on the older two children. All the people go to their house, and Uncle Bill puts us animals back into the barn.

Everybody, I'm sure, wants to talk about the mountain lion in the haunted barn story, but they're afraid to bring it up. It's as if talking about it will somehow make the haunted barn and the ghost mountain lion become a reality.

"Everybody get some good sleep tonight," Elmer announces. "Tomorrow will be a beautiful day, and I'm sure we'll have lots of fun with our guests."

I curl up in my own corner, but I don't plan on sleeping. Max cuddles up to Benny. I wonder if Max really thinks Benny is going to keep him any safer. Benny, of course, falls asleep, once again showing he's not worthy to be a guard dog. That only makes my work tonight easier.

***

Once everybody is asleep, I sneak out of the barn to the people's house. Only a few lights are on in the house. Because of Pearl, Uncle Bill has installed pet doors. This allows me to sneak in with ease. The interior of the house is completely wood. Large, wooden beams run crossways over head.

This is perfect for cats.

I climb up onto one. It gives me a perfect bird's eye view. I wish my people had a house like this so that I don't have to lower myself to interaction with people. Uncle Bill, Aunt Susie, my big man person, and my big woman person are drinking and talking in the kitchen.

"Oh, that old story about the haunted barn," Uncle Bill's deep voice booms. "It is just something I tell the kids to keep them away. That old barn is so decrepit and unsafe. It will probably be torn down soon, anyways."

"We would hate for somebody to step on a rusty old nail," Aunt Susie says.

"I have heard a mountain lion in these parts," Uncle Bill says, "but it has not been for several years now."

"Despite your scary campfire story," the big woman person says, "the kids have fallen fast asleep. Apparently the story wasn't too scary." The people continue talking as I keep looking for Pearl.

She was not at the weenie roast, but why? I slink along the overhead wooden beams to one of the back rooms. There I see Pearl. She lies on a nice doggy cushion. She looks like she's trying to sleep, continually repositioning herself on the cushion. But I can see, even from up here, that she is crying. I can hear her sobs. Now is the time to use my feminine charm, assure her that she is my best friend, and discover what troubles this dear poodle, Pearl.

***

"My dear, friend," I say, just loud enough to catch Pearl's attention. "Why are you crying?"

Pearl's body trembles as she sobs. Has something truly tragic occurred, or is her hair not curling properly?

"It's gone. It's gone. It is simply gone," Pearl says through her sniffles with a high-pitched fake British accent. "My precious! It is simply gone, and I don't know where it could've run off to. Who would dare do such a thing to me? Who would steal my love and joy?"

"I am sorry to hear something has gone wrong," I say. "You don't deserve such a horrible thing; you deserve so much better. You deserve *everything*."

"It was so beautiful, and now it's gone," Pearl says, "and I'm sure there's not another one like it in all the world. I love my diamond-studded collar. I love it so, so, much. And now it's gone."

A diamond-studded collar?

Surely the diamonds are as fake as her accent.

"Without my collar, I am a common dog. Others wouldn't know I deserve a glamorous lifestyle. I'm ashamed to go out without it around my neck. The paparazzi would know something horrible happened."

"Who told you that you are just a mutt without your diamond-studded-collar?" I ask Pearl.

"Nobody has said it," she says, "but I just know it. Everybody would think I'm a mutt if they ever saw me without my diamond-studded collar."

"Everybody thinks that because they want to be like you, the beautiful poodle whom everyone adores." I nearly have to choke down bile as I throw such flattery at Pearl's feet.

"My diamond-studded collar won't make anybody else like me!" Pearl says with a tinge of anger and defiance.

"So it is all the more necessary that your diamond-studded collar be returned to its rightful owner. You," I say. "Otherwise, the diamonds would be wasted."

"But what can I do? I can't bear to be seen without it. I don't have any strength or power. What can I do?"

Yes indeed, what can you do?

"We're both ladies here," I say, "and we are the only ones who understand each other rightly." I pause a second to let the hook sink in. "I will help you out, my dear."

"Thank you, thank you."

I leave Pearl's room, and I sneak along the rafters to head back to the barn. I'm not sure if Pearl was still crying when I left because of sadness over her diamond-studded collar, or if it was out of gratitude for me. I can't help but shake my head as I make my way back into the barn. This mountain lion ghost is silly. I'll never believe in such nonsense. On top of that, there's some mystery animal threatening this farm, and now a bunch of missing diamonds.

After I sneak back into the barn, I approach my sleeping spot, and I see a problem. A hotdog-shaped problem. Benny no longer snuggles with Max. Instead, he waits for me in my sleeping spot. There could be real problems if this overzealous guard dog sounds the alarm by barking. The farm animals already suspect me of being up to no good.

"I've got great news for you, Benny," I say as I sneak up behind him. Benny leaps off the ground an inch, unaware of my approach until I speak to him.

"How can you have good news for me?" he asks. "You wait until Elmer and the others find out you snuck out of the barn—and on your first night here, no less. If you were out plotting with that mountain lion, real or ghost—"

"Pearl said interesting things to me."

"Pearl? *The* Pearl?"

"Of course," I say. "She's my friend now. You're my friend, too, aren't you?"

Benny understands perfectly. He remains quiet and leans in to whisper, "Do you think I have a chance with her?"

"Patience," I tell Benny. "Even magic takes time."

At the mention of magic, Benny turns slightly pale.

"There are no such things as ghost mountain lions," I assure Benny. "I'm talking about the magic of love." I direct Benny back to his sleeping spot where Max sprawls.

Benny doesn't sleep the rest of the night, probably thinking about Pearl. I don't sleep either. I'm making a plan.

CHAPTER 5

The morning announcements from Elmer focus on the day's main activity. The people are going fishing. Uncle Bill will take all three of the children in a boat onto a small lake. I'm surprised when Elmer mentions me.

"Uncle Bill will take Princess and Max. He used to take Alfie with him."

I'm about to object, but Elmer adds, "I'm sure you won't mind eating fresh fish." Elmer is right that I will only get on the boat if I get some tasty fresh fish.

"I must go," Benny shouts out of the crowd to Elmer. "I'll be needed on that boat." Benny must be hoping that Uncle Bill and Aunt Susie will bring Pearl with them on this fishing trip.

"The barn is where we need a guard dog, not on the boat," Elmer says.

About an hour later, Max, Uncle Bill, Aunt Susie with Pearl, the three children, and I are on the boat.

The boat is larger than a rowboat, but Uncle Bill assures the children it's not large enough for anything really fun or serious. I'm thankful there's enough room for me to take a nap in the sun away from everybody casting fishing lines. Uncle Bill's fishing lessons fascinate Max. He wants to play with all the fishing lures.

After a few practice casts, the children are mostly interested in who can cast the farthest.

"You just gotta cast out a ways," Uncle Bill says, "and then you just gotta wait and see what comes."

"What is the fun part?" the youngest girl child asks.

"When you see that bobber in the water dip under, and your fishing line goes straight," Uncle Bill says, "that's when it gets fun. It takes patience, though. Casting your line repeatedly spooks the fish. You gotta wait. Be patient."

That's why I take a nap. I'm waiting patiently for fresh fish.

Amid the fishing and Aunt Susie coddling Pearl, I notice I haven't heard Max in a while. When I know Max is around and I haven't heard him for a while, that's when I get worried. I open one of my eyes half a slit, and I see Max on the edge of the boat. His tail is inside the boat, but he's leaning over as far as he can to look at fish and water bugs. If it wouldn't require me to get up from my nap, I would go over there and "accidentally" nudge him into the lake.

"I think I got one!" Uncle Bill says excitedly. Uncle Bill then explains for everybody listening how to reel in a fish. "I give it a good tug first to make sure the hook is set in the fish's mouth. Then, I reel it in slowly like this. I don't want to do it too fast or too hard so the line doesn't break. Grab that fishing net to scoop it up." There's a soft clicking and whirring sound as Uncle Bill reels his line in. The three children are mesmerized by this angling adventure, and even the boy child has put aside his usually dour mood to cheer it on.

"That looks like a big fish," the boy child says. "Reel it in!"

The boy child grabs the net and leans over eagerly, waiting for the fish to get close. The line dances around as the fish fights for his life. There's some splashing, and then the boy child proudly raises the net in the air.

"Got it!"

His sisters cheer with excitement, and Uncle Bill confirms the catch: "That is a big one."

The fish thrashes around in the net. Uncle Bill ties a line through its mouth and gills, and then he hangs it over the side of the boat.

"Later today I'll show you how to clean fish at home, and then we'll fry them up for dinner," Uncle Bill says.

This first catch makes the children more eager to listen to Uncle Bill's instructions. Throughout the course of the day, they add to their catch. One by one, fish are tied to the string on the side of the boat. I lose count of exactly how many fish they've caught, but I'm sure it will be enough for me. I'll let the people have some, too. Uncle Bill must feel they have caught enough fish, because he comes up with a new plan.

He steers the boat into a forest of reeds. Plants like tall, thick grass reach over the boat as it crawls among the reeds. Frogs, bugs, and even a water snake in the reeds entrance Max and the children.

"It's fun to see the different animals here in the reeds," Uncle Bill says, "but we'll head back home—"

Before Uncle Bill finishes what he is saying, the boat rocks violently. I jump to my feet, wondering what has disturbed my journey. Pearl emits her high-pitched yapping as Aunt Susie protects her in her arms. I hear a loud splash, and I look over to where Max used to be hanging over the side of the boat. He's not there anymore. The people rush over to the side of the boat where the loud splash came from, but I already know that Max is in the lake. I quickly scan the rest of the boat, and opposite where the big splash was, I see a pair of claws reach into the boat. It's no mountain lion; they're far too small. I leap over, hissing and swiping at the claws before they disappear into the water. By now, Pearl yaps furiously from fear.

"All the stress will frizz up my fur! It will frizz up my fur!" Pearl shouts hysterically.

"Where's Max?" the youngest girl child asks.

"Max!" the children call out in unison. I run to the side of the boat where the first splashing noise was. Max is now about six feet behind the boat. He's barely keeping his head above water.

"There he is," the oldest girl child says, pointing at Max.

Uncle Bill pushes the boat back towards Max, and then he grabs the fishing net and pulls Max out of the water. He holds Max up in the air in the fishing net.

"I've never seen such a funny looking furry fish," Uncle Bill jokes. I'm starting to like this Uncle Bill. He's a pretty funny guy. Uncle Bill releases Max back into the boat.

"What happened?" Aunt Susie asks now that Pearl has stopped yapping.

"Don't know," Uncle Bill says, "but I figure Max got a little too curious."

I know that's not right. There was something else with claws that made the boat rock. Max was just a diversion.

When we get back to shore, it is as I feared. Only one complete fish remains on the string. Only the heads of the other fish remain. This baffles the others, but I know the clawed creature is the thief.

Back at the barn, Ned the horse interviews Max. Max claims he was trying to catch a dragonfly, and he thought for sure that he could get it, but he must've underestimated how quickly the dragonfly was moving. I wonder if that clawed creature didn't pull Max into the water. Benny voices his regrets about not being there to protect Pearl. I decide not to tell anybody I know who the culprit is. The clawed creature was sending us a message by just leaving the heads of the fish.

Since there is only one fish, my people greedily keep it for themselves. Before I can get too sour about it, Benny comes over and asks me if I can set up a meeting for him and Pearl.

"It's not the right time for you and Pearl to get together," I tell Benny.

This disappoints him, but I see defiance in his eyes, not resignation.

"A group activity would help her be more comfortable with you at first," I tell Benny. I have not made any progress towards obtaining the diamond-studded collar, and so I need to do something to keep my Benny-and-Pearl plan moving forward.

"I will arrange a group activity to include you and Pearl tomorrow night. Pearl will be there. You make sure you and a few other animals are there. What is something you farm animals do for fun at night?"

Benny doesn't hesitate to say, "Cow tipping."

"Pearl and I will be there," I say without any idea what "cow tipping" is.

***

Pearl is apprehensive about the cow tipping. I peer down from the rafters of Uncle Bill's house again, trying to coax her out.

"Remember, your presence among the other animals will help us discover who stole your diamond-studded collar. Whoever acts odd and avoids you is probably guilty."

"But this is my mansion," Pearl objects, "and I don't spend time with those dirty farm animals."

"Believe me, I know how you feel. But it is part of celebrity status. You can maintain your mystique by staying in your mansion, but unless the common dirty farm animals spot you occasionally in public, they may forget you. Max tells me he's seen on TV many celebrities at sporting events. This is one such sporting event. It will be completely normal for a celebrity of your stature to attend."

"I am still shook up about what happened on the boat," Pearl says. "The paparazzi always scheme to get a look at me."

"Don't worry about that," I say. "To everybody else that was a nuisance. But it yielded a valuable clue to me."

Pearl reluctantly gets up and pads out of her room as I leave. She can leave her house whenever she wants because Uncle Bill and Aunt Susie know Pearl doesn't try to leave. She follows me out the pet doors, and I lead her away from Uncle Bill's house and barn to a larger cow pasture. Beyond that, I see yet another barn, but it appears abandoned.

Max and Benny wait by the entrance of the large cow pasture.

"Where's everybody else?" I ask Benny as I approach him, a few paces ahead of Pearl.

"Everybody else is asleep," Benny says. "Besides, I can't exactly ask Daisy the cow to join us for cow tipping."

I look around the large cow pasture, and there are about twenty-four cows. A few of them lie down, but most of them stand. Except for a few twitching tails, they're completely still.

I hop on the top rail of the fence, and I look over the attendance for the cow-tipping event. There's only Max, Pearl, and Benny. This is disheartening.

Before I start my speech, Max says, "This fencepost tastes horrible," scrunching up his nose. I don't bother asking why Max is biting the fence post.

"Thank you all for joining me at this illustrious event," I announce. No applause comes. Benny is close to Pearl, gazing sideways at her. Pearl looks up into the sky, pretending that she is somewhere else. Max licks a different area of the post. "I have asked Benny to explain the event to us. Benny, why don't you come up here and explain cow tipping?"

Benny looks at me as if to say, "Who, me?"

"Ahem, yes, of course," Benny says as he walks towards the fencepost I am standing on.

Benny turns around to face his audience.

"Cow tipping is a simple, yet fun, sport. Notice that all of these cows are sleeping. The ones who are standing, well, all you have to do is run up to them, leap into them and give them a good strong push. They will fall right over in a heap of cow meat. It is hilarious."

Benny chuckles to himself, but the others and I don't see how this is funny.

"Max," I say to the audience. "You're up first."

"I suggest that easier one over there," Benny says. One cow stands slightly outside the group. We all make our way along the perimeter of the fence, and Max trots carefully over to the cow.

"What do I do?" Max whispers, looking back to us.

Benny gives a pushing motion with his front paws.

Instead, Max licks the cow a few times. I have no idea what Max is thinking as he licks the cow. Then Max puts his two front paws on the rear leg of the cow. To nobody's surprise, the cow does nothing.

"You have to run and then jump to push the cow," Benny whispers from the fence to Max.

Max backs up several paces, runs, leaps, and smashes into the side of the cow. Max falls down, barely landing on his feet. The cow does not budge.

"A few more tries will do the trick," Benny reassures us. "Again," Benny urges. Benny looks over to Pearl and says, "This sure is a blast, isn't it?"

Pearl doesn't recognize that Benny is talking to her, and I fear Benny is starting to think my plan was a bad idea. He will go back to the barn and tell Elmer about me sneaking out of the barn the other night.

Max makes another running leap at the cow. Once again, there is no affect other than Max's bruised ego, and Benny more deeply questioning this whole plan of mine.

"Third try is a charm," I urge Max.

Max comes over to us at the fence and says, "I think this whole cow tipping sport is fake. Like wrestling."

"Give it one more try," I tell Max, "and if it doesn't work, Benny will try—since it was *his* idea." If not, and he gets embarrassed in front of Pearl, who cares? He's going to tell Elmer anyways.

Max looks me in the eyes as if to say, "I really have to try again?"

"Max," I say to encourage him, "you played a vital role in defeating the wicked coyote, Snarl. I'm sure you can tip a cow over."

Max grits his teeth, turns towards the cow, and he crouches down. He wiggles his behind slightly, and his tail twitches. I know from experience that this is Max's favorite position when he is ready for a vicious attack.

Before Max pounces, a long, drawn-out howl from a dog reverberates from the nearby forest. The cows don't notice, but all of us aspiring cow-tippers go on full alert. Max pops up out of his crouch, and Benny growls under his breath.

"I'll protect you," Benny promises Pearl.

"I knew I should have stayed at home," Pearl says, disregarding Benny's devotion. "I do have my nails to work on."

Another howl comes from the forest, and, for once, Benny's guard dog act becomes helpful.

"That's a howl from a happy hunting hound," he informs us. "It's no threat. Somebody is out hunting in the forest, and the hunting dog is tracking the scent."

"Okay, Max," I say to Max, eager to get this spectacle back on track, "knock that cow into tomorrow."

Max resumes his crouch.

His behind wiggles, his tail twitches, and he focuses on a large white spot on the broad side of the cow. He rushes and leaps at the cow.

The next few seconds seem to pass in slow motion. The night sky and everything around us lights up as if it's day for a split second; Max is caught as if by a camera flash just as his fleshy fur impacts into the side of the cow. Immediately following the flash, the sky seems to have split in two from a thunderclap that makes all of us leap into the air.

The lightning strike and thunder wake the cows. The next phase of my slow motion lightning strike is the dumping rain. The raindrops feel like they are the size of the ping-pong balls the kids love to have Max chase around my house. The lightning strike plus the torrential downpour scares the cows, and now the group of them rushes towards Max in a stampede.

Max stands dazed. He didn't manage to move the cow one centimeter, let alone tip it over. The cow runs headlong towards the forest beyond the fence. All of the other cows are not far behind.

I rush at Max to pull him out of the way of the stampede.

"We need to get out of here!"

I pull on Max, and he has enough sense to follow me. I have no choice but to lead us towards the forest because the stampeding cows block our way back.

When we reach the fence, we discover that the first cow broke it open. The other cows stampeding behind us will soon follow us into the forest. Each raindrop soaks my fur more deeply, and I'm sure I appear to have been completely submerged. I look over at Max as we race into the forest, and he is also soaked. I want to stop, but Max runs straight ahead as fast as he can. I guess there's no reason to stop yet.

I stay with Max stride for stride until we enter a forest clearing with a creek running through it. The rain slows. We have found a campsite with two tents down in a ravine. The stampeding cows won't follow us down here. I hear people approaching through the forest, probably to get out of the rain.

I have a feeling it's the teenage boys with a hunting dog.

***

"Back in the tents!" a teenage boy calls out to his buddies. Max and I hide in a nearby bush before the teenage boys enter the campsite.

The boy who shot at me with a slingshot hurries to a tent, and a handful of other boys follow. The first boy carries something I recognize. It's not a BB gun pistol. It's bigger. It's a rifle. I know that if I face this boy again, he will kill me with his rifle.

"What about Dan?" one of the other boys asks.

"Dan's fine," the first one insists.

Once the teenage boys are zipped up inside their tents, I tell Max, "Let's get away from these boys." Max sees the rifle, too, because he doesn't hesitate to follow me.

"We just have to watch out for whomever Dan is," I tell Max as we hurry downstream in the direction of Uncle Bill's house. This must be the same creek that goes by the thicket David the goat was in. The cows' feet pound the ground outside the ravine, and so Max and I stay down in the ravine as we head downstream.

After a few minutes, we hear a loud splash downstream, and we freeze in our tracks.

I stand like a statue, only rotating my ears slightly and gazing around with my eyes. It's only then that I notice I'm shivering from being soaking wet. I look over at Max, and he looks like one sad cat. I almost feel pity for him.

Sensing no imminent danger, I say to Max, "Keep moving. The sooner we do, the sooner we'll get clean and dry."

"Won't our people come find us?" Max pleads wishfully.

"They don't know we're out here," I remind Max. "We didn't exactly tell everybody we were going cow tipping. We can't leave the ravine yet because we'll get trampled by one of those cows we're supposed to tip over, and we can't head back upstream to the campsite. You saw the gun that boy had."

I take a few steps, and Max reluctantly follows. We go around a bend, and I see a furry beast somewhat larger than me floating down the stream. The moonlight illuminates his brown and black fur. Something sparkles on his tail. My blood goes colder when I see that the furry beast is exactly what I had feared: it's a giant raccoon.

The boys must have been hunting that raccoon.

But where's the dog, Dan?

"Dan... Dan..." the boys call out from the campsite. They've left their tents and are moving closer. Their yells distract the raccoon, and he wobbles, struggling to keep his balance on his river raft.

ROAR!

Between us and the boys' campsite, the ferocious mountain lion roar shatters the night. The raccoon leaps into the air and splashes into the water. He scurries to the far shore and disappears into the forest.

To my shock, a golden dog surfaces and paddles to the near shore. He coughs up water and gasps as he pulls himself up on the bank. He's about knee-high on a person. This must be Dan. The raccoon was trying to drown Dan.

Dan staggers to his feet, and I fear he catches a whiff of me and Max in the air, but he obediently heads towards his owner's voice. How can he not sense the mountain lion? His tail sags between his legs.

"Keep moving downstream," I urge Max. I don't have to persuade Max to put more distance between us, the rifle toting teenage boys, and the mountain lion.

We move warily, but I can't help but grin to myself because I know where Pearl's diamond-studded collar is.

It's on the ringed tail of that giant raccoon.

***

We stumble clumsily down the ravine, eager to reach Uncle Bill's warm barn. The rain stops after a few minutes, and I can see to my right what must be the haunted barn Uncle Bill talked about at the campfire. After a flash of lightning, the thunder doesn't arrive for several seconds. A white layer peeks out from the old red paint on the barn. One of the doors hangs crooked on its hinges so that even though it is closed, there is a gap at the bottom large enough for me.

"You think that's the haunted barn Uncle Bill was talking about?" Max says.

"I'm sure it is," I tell Max, "but I'm also sure it's not haunted." I need to give Max all the confidence that I can at this point until we get back to Uncle Bill's house.

"Let's just get out of here," Max says anxiously.

Now that the rain has stopped, Dan's barking commences from upstream.

The teenage boys yell out in the distance. "Go get him, Dan! Go get him!"

I don't know if they're hunting that giant raccoon, or if they're hunting me and Max, but I don't care. Max and I take a few more steps down the ravine.

ROAR!

The mountain lion's roar sounds out again. The mountain lion must be claiming all these woods as its territory because we've heard it behind us by the campsite, and now we've heard it in front of us, between us and Uncle Bill's house.

Considering that the old barn isn't haunted, it is much safer than a real mountain lion. I veer right towards the haunted barn.

"Come on," I tell Max, "you don't stand a chance against a mountain lion."

"Oh, I hate this, I hate this," Max says as he follows me to the barn.

We squeeze under the door and enter complete darkness. Even as cats, I can't see a thing. Clouds must be blocking the moon. There is a strange scent of animals that I can't quite recognize, but this doesn't alarm me. It is a barn, after all; who knows what animals have been living here?

But is it the raccoon's lair? My fur raises on my back.

Max and I sit still by the doorway.

"Nobody's home," Max whispers to me.

Silence envelops us in the barn for several more seconds. I swear I smell something I recognize, but I'm not sure.

The cacophony of hunting noises continues outside, but we haven't heard the mountain lion again.

Perhaps the teenage boys are hunting the mountain lion.

"I don't know why," Max says, "but I think we need to get out of here. We haven't heard the mountain lion again, and this barn sure is scaring me."

"The barn isn't haunted," I tell Max. "After the campfire, I snuck into Uncle Bill's house. He told the big man person and the big woman person that he tells those stories to keep the kids away. Uncle Bill himself said that it's not dangerous. You are safe here. I promise."

I'm not able to shake the feeling that there is something familiar about this barn, but I direct my attention to the outside. I peek out from the small entryway, and I hear rustling in the bushes to our left. Dan breaks through the bushes towards the barn. He doesn't see us. He presses his nose to the ground as if his nostrils are vacuuming up our scent.

Four teenage boys soon follow out of the bushes. They stop when they see the barn. Perhaps they've heard stories about it, too. The leader of the teenage boys readies his rifle. The boys cautiously approach the barn, and Dan comes with them. I hope the boy realizes that a rifle is no good against ghosts.

Dan is unwilling to enter. He wags his tail, and it batters against the barn as he sniffs. He works his way along the outside of it. Only an old rotted barn wall made of ancient wooden slats separate us from Dan. As of yet, he's not brave enough to stick his nose under the door. I extend my claws to slash his snout if he changes his mind.

With my back against the wall and Dan inches away, I look around the inside of the old barn again. I still can't really see anything, but I sense something. I sense something that I haven't sensed since… Since…

"Come on!" the boys all yell out to each other as they run around the barn. "Let's find them! Let's get them!"

I peek out the small entrance, and I see the sneakers of teenage boys go by every few seconds. I don't know what to tell Max. If we run out of the barn, that dog Dan will get us. Besides, we can't outrun a rifle.

Maybe one of us could get away. The other would have to sacrifice themself for the one who gets away. I can't ask Max to do that for me, and I certainly can't leave Max to rule my domain. He's not ready. But we can't stay here.

"Max," I whisper. "We need to hide somewhere in the barn. Let's look."

"Are you crazy? This place is scary as anything. I'm more afraid of what could be inside of this barn than I am of what I know is outside the barn."

Walking into the interior of the barn, I'm only able to see a little bit in front of me because of how dark it is. The rain clouds must continue to block the moonlight. I reach a steep wooden staircase. It must go up to a hayloft. A hayloft will be as good a place as any to hide. If I'm lucky, maybe there will be things up there I can push down off the hayloft and onto the boys so we can get away. I put my front paw on the lower step of the wooden staircase. I feel Max quaking next to me. It's as if my first step onto the staircase is a cue to the feline gods. Just as I place my foot on the step, a flash of lightning, immediately followed by thunder, breaks the dark silence. Rain commences in buckets. It sounds like golf balls are pelting the barn roof, and rain comes through the cracks and on to us.

"The rain will distract and slow the boys," Max says. "Let's make a run for Uncle Bill's."

"No, Max," I whisper. "There's something here for me." I take a few more steps up the stairs, not sure exactly what awaits, but I sense there's something. I won't spend the rest of my life wondering, "What if I had gone up the stairs?"

CHAPTER 6

I start up the steps. Once my paw touches the fourth step, a light clicks on upstairs in the back of the hayloft. I freeze.

"Don't go up there," Max whispers to me. "Let's get out of here." Without answering, I go up another step. I'm drawn to whatever I sense up there. The light pulls me in as if it is the whirring of a can opener opening a can of cat food.

My finely honed feline instincts register a slight breeze, and it's caused by another cat, flying through the air at me. From my left side, a brawny cat swoops in. I duck out of the way just in time so that I miss the brunt of his attack. I hear his jaws snap shut. He is now on the right side of the staircase, and I've shifted to the left. He uses his hind legs to push off of the wall; he aims to push me off the staircase, but I leap up to the next step, and he flies past the staircase.

Before I catch my breath, another cat flies at me. This one is small and agile. These two must have planned to work in tandem. One of them is big and strong, and the other is small and fast. This quick one does not miss, and his jaws clamp on to my fur. I let out a screech. These cats are no average house cats. My twisting and hissing doesn't scare them away. The larger cat returns and lunges on top of me. He uses his girth to hold me down as the other cat makes veterinary-like incisions with his claws and fangs.

Since Max barely has the skill to walk on a fence without falling over, it never crosses my mind that Max could help, but from somewhere deep in his primordial instincts, Max turns from a bumbling orange and white house cat into a beast fighting for survival.

Max lets out a yell and tears into the two attacking cats who are pinning me down. They did not expect Max to attack, either. They must have sensed Max's weakness. All three of us turn out to be wrong. Max spins and slashes with rage as he hisses and howls. This allows me to free myself and rejoin the fight. I don't feel any pain from my injuries yet, and Max and I fight side by side to send the smaller cat fleeing up into the lit hayloft. The large cat is able to twist away from us after we inflict some deep scratches on him, and he flees away, after his companion and up into the hayloft.

"Max…" I say, and as I look at him I see him turned as if from an orange and white tiger back into a simple house cat. He seems as bewildered as I am by his transformation. "You saved my life."

"Let's get out of—"

"Princess." A deep husky voice rings throughout the barn, cutting Max off. "You have indeed grown strong."

"How do the ghosts—who supposedly don't exist—know your name?" Max asks.

I realize what I have been sensing this whole time, and I know it must be up in the hayloft. The light in the hayloft shows a silhouette of a large cat.

"Patches?" I say, more to myself than anybody else.

***

For the first time since I started up the staircase, the pounding of the rain registers in my ears. A dim light illuminates the downstairs. Pairs of green and yellow eyes light up around Max and me in the barn.

This is not the raccoon's lair.

This is Patches' lair.

My heart pounds, but not because of the sneak attack. My heart pounds because of the presence of Patches. I want to see his face. I have not seen it for years. I have only dreamed of it.

Patches fulfills my dreams, but not in the way I expect.

As Patches starts down the steps towards me, he says, "You have indeed become strong, but not strong enough."

Before I know what is happening, Patches leaps down at me, swipes with his front paw and knocks me off the staircase. Max comes to my side. I know I have never faced a beast so strong. One-Eyed Jack or Snarl the coyote are close, but I expected them to be powerful. I don't expect Patches to be so terrifying.

While I'm still bewildered by this new attack, Patches leaps down again and bats me around. He dispatches Max with one kick of his hind leg, and Max thuds against the barn wall. I try to dodge Patches, but he's too fast. He has strength, weight, and agility that I've never encountered. He bats me from side to side a few times with his front paws. I realize that he is toying with me as I would a mouse.

I try to attack, and so does Max, but Patches fends off all of our attacks with ease.

Max and I lie huddled together, scratched and wounded, breathing deeply. There is no way we can defeat this enemy. I look around at the on-looking cats. There are at least a dozen pairs of eyes, all loyal to Patches, gazing on us.

Instead of continuing to toy with us, Patches says, "If it makes you feel any better, that is the best fight any cat has ever put up." Patches scoots back and sits up straight. "Get up, Princess and Max."

Max and I sit up as best we can, but it is difficult with all of our injuries.

"I have also heard how you defeated that horrible coyote, Snarl."

It's not best to tell Patches that Snarl was mostly killed thanks to Max's foolishness. For once, Max is wise enough to keep his mouth shut.

Patches continues: "You may join me and my minions in our quest to usher in a new epoch of history." I narrow my eyes, and Patches senses my question.

"A new age when cats will rule, but without people."

***

"Without people?" I ask. "Don't misunderstand me. I generally loathe people, but I do derive some small sense of satisfaction from being their ruler. I help them by giving them a sense of purpose and meaning in their life. Although we may view it as menial to pack our cans of food, open them for us, and clean the litter box, for most people, that's the best purpose they can have in life."

"What about the mountain lion?" Max pipes up without my approval.

Patches looks at me first before he looks at Max for a brief second. Although I am certain this is Patches—he has his namesake patches of brown, black, white, and orange fur—he also has an injured eye. Scars mar his fur coat. He is unnaturally large for a house cat.

His offer to rule the world without people entices me, but I would prefer to rule in luxury, not as a tribal leader in a primitive barn.

"People aren't your only enemies, remember," I tell Patches. "Surely you have recently heard the mountain lion, and there is another secret enemy lurking in the forest," I say without revealing my knowledge of the giant raccoon. "Don't forget those teenage boys. I'm sure you've noticed they have a gun. A large one. A rifle. Without that rainstorm, they would be beating down your door."

"We have many enemies," Patches says in agreement. He betrays no fear from anything I mentioned. "That secret enemy that you speak of, lurking in the forest, is a mere raccoon."

I attempt to hide my surprise.

"And this raccoon is an ally of mine," Patches says.

"You need allies other than cats?" I challenge Patches.

"He is a temporary ally. This raccoon is the infamous 'Ninja Coon.' He has evaded hunting dogs for years while growing large and wealthy."

Wealthy enough to have a diamond-studded collar on his tail.

"I have permitted the Ninja Coon to become wealthy and powerful as my ally for now," Patches says, "but as soon as Uncle Bill's farm animals are weak enough, I will dispatch of the Ninja Coon, just as I will all my enemies."

"I have no doubt you can handle a raccoon just as I have handled coyotes," I say, to display my power, "but don't underestimate teenage boys with guns. They can be destructive, nasty, and unpredictable—perhaps their most dangerous trait."

"We will soon attack those boys and take their rifle. You will see."

"What about the mountain lion?" Max asks again.

Patches chuckles.

"I don't think I understand the joke," Max says quietly.

I steal a few glances around the barn. Many of the cat eyes have moved in closer. I can now see they are tough cats, much like Patches. Not as large, but certainly more formidable than an average house cat.

"The mountain lion is no enemy," Patches announces.

"Just because the mountain lion is a distant cousin of ours," I begin to warn Patches, "don't think he will follow your plan to rule the world without people."

"This mountain lion does not have to be persuaded. *We* are the mountain lion. The mountain lion is a group of my own cats who have learned to 'roar' in unison and harmony, and this results in a roar that sounds like a mountain lion. We have used it to scare others away from our territory, and—"

"And you've used it to steer us into this barn," I say.

"Exactly," Patches says. "Come. Let me show you around."

There are about two dozen cats on this lower level. Seven other cats look down from the hayloft. I can only guess that these seven cats are Patches' chief advisers.

Patches struts around the lower level of the barn. Max and I make quick eye contact, and I sense that Max is counting on me to protect him.

Patches leads us into the next room, which is under the hayloft. Hay bales and wood logs are arranged in an obstacle course. Cats bite and scratch at each other, practicing their fighting. I notice they fight without hissing. This is a combat training room for cats.

"Secrecy is our weapon," Patches tells me. "We learn how to attack without the typical hissing and meowing. If we need to, as I already mentioned, we can meow to make others think a mountain lion is in pursuit."

"Everybody is a male cat," I observe, not betraying any judgment.

"You are right," Patches says, "and that is not by accident. For now, the reality is that we need an army to conquer people. Even though I have more than twenty-four soldiers in my command, and that is enough to take over Uncle Bill's farm, more will be needed. Female cats, accordingly, bear kittens to enlarge the army. Once we have taken over sizable territories, then of course the female cats will have a role other than just bearing kittens."

I bite my lip to hide my disgust. I don't want to know where the female cats bearing kittens are right now. It would anger me.

"You, however," Patches says, "cannot have kittens." Patches speaks casually.

How does he know?

"Your owners once took you to the vet. The veterinarian fixed you so that you cannot have kittens. Your owners didn't have your consent. They know they must suppress our numbers, lest we revolt."

I confess, I hate it when my people forcefully take me to the vet.

"Princess and Max," Patches says gently, "you must join me. Work with me against Uncle Bill's farm. Against the people who take you to the vet. Will you join me?"

This is an offer I can't refuse, disguised as a request.

"I will join you," I lie to Patches, "but you must tell me why you want to get rid of people as our servants."

***

"You have so much potential," Patches tells me, "but you need to see reality. You have been living a lie."

I narrow my eyes in disbelief at Patches.

Patches' anger boils over, and he yells at me, "Cats are not really in charge! We have just been blinded by our own self-love to convince ourselves that we are in charge."

Patches paces back and forth now, fuming with anger.

"What are you talking about?" I ask.

"Tell me one thing people are good for," Patches snaps at me without hesitation.

"They sleep in my bed at night to keep it warm for me," I say.

Patches rolls his eyes.

"That isn't your bed. That is your owner's bed. It is their house, and it is their bed. People everywhere sleep in their bed at night, and since they don't need it during the day, they let you sleep on it."

I have to admit I had never thought of it that way before.

"Many people even put extra towels or blankets on parts of the bed so that your fur does not get on their bed," Patches says, with emphasis on the word "their."

"What about the food they work so hard for, can for me, and then give to me each and every evening, even though there is plenty of game to catch myself?" I ask.

"People don't spend all day making food for you," Patches says. "People spend most of their waking hours working for something they call 'money.' Money is a mysterious thing, or concept, really, that they exchange for power, time, and goods and services. They use that money for themselves. They use a tiny fraction of their money to buy your food from a place they call 'the store.' Haven't you noticed that their kitchen is full of food for themselves, but your cans of food only take up a sliver of space in their whole house?"

Again, I had never thought of it from this perspective.

"But they have special heaters for me," I say. "They even have one that I am able to sleep on, and they sit and look at me adoringly for hours."

"What do they call this heater?" Patches asks. Skepticism drips from his question.

"TV."

Patches chuckles again, and he looks to the other cats surrounding us.

"She thinks that the TV is a heater for her. Ridiculous."

Patches shakes his head, and some of his advisers venture a smirk.

Patches explains: "A TV is a piece of technology that people have developed over decades. Most cats have discovered that the TV actually shows small moving pictures, and people are mesmerized by watching. The heat is simply a byproduct of their machine showing them moving pictures and sounds. Have you ever blocked the view between them and their TV? Does your tail ever droop down?"

"Sometimes," I admit.

"And when your tail droops down, they get upset, and they force you to move it. You can't lay however you want. The people demand to watch their TV how they want, and they don't allow you to put your tail where you want. They allow you to rest on top of the television because it doesn't interfere with their TV watching, but that's all."

"What about those large portable heaters they call cars?" I dare to ask, afraid that Patches will again turn my conception of the world upside down.

"Cars do provide heat for you," Patches admits, "but like a TV, that is a byproduct. Like TVs, cars are machines that people have developed for themselves. Humans are slow and lazy. They can't move quickly like us. They are dependent on these machines. Cars are actually very dangerous for animals. They are responsible for killing many cats each and every day. You see, far from being portable heaters, cars are actually cat-killing machines."

"Yes," I say, "cars are dangerous." I think back to the handful of times my big man person almost ran me over while backing out of my garage.

Patches knows he is winning the debate, and so he presses his point home.

"And what of new pets?" Patches asks. "You don't choose what other pets come into your domain, do you? If a nearby house gets a new kitten or puppy, do you have any say in that? If not, are you really in control?"

"No," I concede.

"I suspect you didn't want this frumpy orange and white cat, Max, did you?"

Patches looks Max up and down. Max shrinks back, trying to hide behind me. I turn to look at Max, and I see his eyes full of fear, and I want to show him pity, but I know that I cannot show any weakness in front of Patches.

Max is a fool, but he is my fool.

"What about veterinarians?" I say. "Ultimately, we need them."

"Those veterinarians may have a small role to play in the New Age," Patches says. "However, it is better if only strong cats survive. Ultimately, veterinarians undermine feline control by reducing our numbers through forced sterilization and by allowing sick and weak cats to live. I am convinced that once us cats rule the world, we will learn the same veterinarian skills. Besides, without people, we won't need veterinarians to heal injuries from people."

I immediately think of the rifle-toting teenagers. I also think of Todd, the whole reason I ended up at Uncle Bill's farm. Patches is right: much feline suffering is at the hands of people. And yet, I can't submit to Patches' scheme.

The only way to defeat Patches is to play along with him for now. If I refuse, he won't let me leave alive.

I nod my head in agreement.

"It is agreed then?" Patches says. "I am giving you an incredible opportunity. You will work with me to rule in this New Age."

The tone in his voice tells me I have no choice other than to agree.

"Yes, I will work with you," I lie to Patches. I know that Patches is not only wrong about whether or not we need people, but Patches is also wrong about one other key thing. I am Princess, the empress of my domain, and I don't share my rule with anybody, not even Patches.

I only need to pretend to work with Patches long enough to cross him.

***

"My only question now," Patches says, "is whether or not your sidekick Max will join us." Patches tilts his head as he looks at Max, who cowers behind me.

"Don't do this, Princess," Max whispers to me. "It's not right."

I know it's not right, but I can't tell Max that now. We need to play along so we have a chance to cross Patches later.

"This is our chance," I tell Max, "to fulfill our destiny."

"Exactly," says Patches.

Max lets out a sniffle and starts to cry. He presses in closer behind me, hoping to make himself invisible and avoid the situation.

"We all know you're still there, Max," Patches says. "You can't hide from destiny. Will you join us or not?"

I move over to expose Max, but he moves with me.

"Come out and face me like a real cat," Patches commands.

"No," Max squeaks.

"What was that?" Patches asks. Patches' advisers stand ready to attack Max. They are eager to do so.

"I said no."

Why can't Max follow along and do what I do?

Patches exchanges glances with his advisers and nods toward Max. Two of them come over, grab Max, and push him down before Patches.

"Let me be clear," Patches says. "You don't have a choice. If you are not with me, then you are against me."

Max lies low for a few seconds, but then he does something amazing. Max rises up and sits tall.

Has Max grown this much since he came to my house as a kitten?

I soon discover he has not grown in intelligence.

Max locks eyes with Patches.

"Let me be equally clear," Max says. "I am against you."

The advisers' bodies tense during a few seconds of silence. I wonder if Patches ever considered the possibility that somebody like Max would resist him.

"So be it. Don't say I did not give you a chance," Patches says. "I will show my never-ending mercy, for even though you deserve the harshest punishment for betrayal, I will extend mercy. You are hereby sentenced to an indefinite amount of physical training for re-education."

I have no idea what re-education means, but the advisers know what this means, and smiles spread over their faces.

"Take him away," Patches commands.

I make eye contact with Max, and his eyes speak more to me than he ever said with words: "Don't leave me. Stay with me. Protect me. You have always been my empress."

Patches' advisers take Max away.

My stomach burns with indignation from losing one of my subjects to Patches. I can't let that show. Rather, it motivates me all the more to defeat Patches. But to do that, I must wait. I must wait for the perfect time.

"Don't worry," Patches says to me after Max is out of sight. "It may be difficult now, but we all must make sacrifices for the greater good. You will be surprised at how effective our re-education is. If he survives, that is."

Patches starts pacing about the barn.

"You will be key in moving forward to get rid of Uncle Bill and Aunt Susie," Patches explains.

"They aren't where we should start," I tell Patches.

"You have a plan?" Patches asks, cocking his head towards me with interest.

"The farm is the goal, but there are intermediate steps. We need to get the Ninja Coon before the teenage boys get him."

"What for? I can get rid of that old beast any time I want. I may need him to help get the rifle from those boys."

"It's simple," I explain. "That coon has a diamond-studded collar around his tail. He stole it from Pearl. It is the key to her heart. Pearl is the key to Aunt Susie's and Benny the guard dog's heart. Whoever has the diamond-studded collar therefore has the keys to the kingdom."

"Cunning," Patches agrees. "I will tell you where the Ninja Coon's lair is. Go back to the farm for the day and make sure nobody is alarmed by Max's disappearance. We can't have those people searching the forest for Max now."

"For the greater good, I will endure the farm this day," I tell Patches.

After Patches describes the Ninja Coon's lair, I exit the barn alone through the dilapidated doorway that I entered hours ago with Max. I go towards Uncle Bill's farm.

CHAPTER 7

I return to Uncle Bill's farm as the sun comes up. I expect the farm animals to be asleep, but everybody is awake and full of energy.

"Where's Max?" Benny demands.

"Out playing," I say nonchalantly. I've rehearsed this conversation repeatedly in my head since I left Patches.

"It's not safe out there," Elmer says. "Make sure your people search for him in the woods."

"Don't worry," I reassure all of the farm animals, who wait to hear what I have to say. However, I don't know what Benny told them about the thunderstorm and stampede late last night.

"My people are overly protective of Max. If they feel the need to find him, my people can do that. But, trust me, Max is playing with bugs." During a few seconds of silence, I wonder if they believe me. For some reason, these animals don't seem to trust me.

"There have been reports of an alleged stampede in the far cow pasture," Ned the interviewing horse says. "Tell our viewers what you witnessed."

"Max and I were with Benny," I say, to make sure they understand that Benny was with me, "and a flash of lightning startled the cattle. They panicked into a stampede."

"Is it true that the rushing bovines trampled Max?" Ned asks.

"Bovine is a fancy word for cow," Daisy interjects.

"I know what a bovine is," I say, "and Max was not trampled. The cows stampeded, and Max and I had nowhere to go but into the forest. As nocturnal cats, we enjoy the woods at night. Max enjoys it so much, he stayed behind to play with bugs."

"A startling turn of events," Ned comments. "What viewers want to know is, why you were at the far cow pasture in the first place? If you had stayed in the barn as Elmer instructed, then there would have been no death by trampling."

"There was a stampede, but everybody got away safely."

"And what were you doing there?" Ned says, his eyebrows slanting.

Before I answer, Benny jumps in.

"As the guard dog over the facility in question," Benny says to the group, "I took Princess and Max on a late night patrol for two purposes. Firstly, they needed to be oriented to the whole area, including the far cow pasture. Since they are nocturnal, I thought it would be wisest to do so at night. There is no way I could have known that a fierce thunderclap would send the cows into a stampede. Secondly, Princess and Max are naturally good at protecting territories, and so I thought it would be best to enlist their help against this phantom invader."

The other animals exchange glances, unsure whether I should be in trouble for disobeying Elmer's orders, or if Benny should be in trouble for disobeying Elmer's orders. Elmer glares at Benny, clearly displeased.

"I have a question." Daisy the cow speaks up. "Now that you've seen the whole farm, would you recommend that Uncle Bill and Aunt Susie sell this farm to the real estate developer? We would lose our home, but it would be a financial windfall for Uncle Bill and Aunt Susie."

What is Daisy talking about?

"Honestly…" I say, finding the word unnatural.

"Interesting question," Elmer says, "but did you encounter the mountain lion?"

The crowd of animals falls silent, and all eyes turn to me.

"I suppose we heard a mountain lion," I say, "but if you are clever like us cats, you can keep away. The mountain lion is a distant cousin. The mountain lion's roar means, 'Stay away.' It's not as though the mountain lion hunts for us."

Of course, this is not true about Patches and his gang, but I don't foresee anybody else entering the forest.

"Another question," Ned the interviewing horse interjects. "Why did you stay in the rain all night?"

I don't blink, but I start to sweat a little as Ned nearly catches me in a lie.

"There are dry spots under dense branches and overhanging rocks," I tell Ned. "But I have something more important to tell you."

I need to change the subject quickly.

"While in the woods," I continue, "I gained valuable clues about this phantom attacker who has been invading the farm. I know who has been stealing chicken eggs, and fish off the line."

"Who is it?" everybody asks in unison.

"I'm not completely sure, and so I will have to spend more time in the woods to confirm the phantom's identity. Once confirmed, we will need to come up with a plan to conquer it, if I have not already done so on my own."

"Who is it?" the animals press.

"Elmer would agree that I shouldn't accuse anybody until I have enough evidence," I say. "Otherwise, it would unnecessarily throw you into a panic, and it would be unfair to the accused. Elmer, give me more time in the forest to confirm the identity of the phantom menace."

"You may have more time in the forest," Elmer says, "but bring Max back. He can't spend time however he pleases while on my farm."

I know better than to push Elmer further.

"That's it for now, everybody," Elmer says, addressing all the farm animals. "Everything is back to normal."

Benny comes up to me to talk privately.

"That was ingenious of you, Princess," Benny says. "Intentionally causing a stampede so that I would have to save Pearl. Brilliant. I did hurt my leg a little bit, but overall I'm okay."

"I'm going to go out again to talk with Pearl to help you," I say. I smile at my stroke of luck. Benny thinks the stampede was part of my plan that helped him spend more time with Pearl.

I make my way over to Uncle Bill's house, and I sneak in. I go to Pearl's room. She is pacing nervously.

"How are you doing, Pearl?" I ask. "Benny was brave to save you."

"I am never leaving this house again," Pearl says in a shrill voice, without acknowledging Benny's heroics. This is not going well. She will have to leave this house at some point if I'm ever going to help Benny win her over.

"That was a troubling evening," I say, "but Benny saved you, and with a little time, I think you'll be ready for more celebrity appearances."

Pearl continues pacing and muttering to herself. I hope that time is all she needs, but not too much time. As I go back to the barn, I look over to the forest. I wonder how Max is doing, but the forest betrays no answer.

***

I spend the rest of the day acting as natural as I can. I don't know if I'm paranoid, but I think the other animals sensed something is not quite right, that I'm not telling the truth. They would be right about that. I can't tell the truth. Not about Patches, and certainly not about Max. Once I get the diamond-studded collar and set everything right, then they can learn most of the truth. None of them can handle the truth right now. Responsibility comes with being an empress like me, and the average animal simply cannot understand that.

At night, once everybody is snoring, I give Benny a wink and leave the barn for the forest. He thinks I'm working to win Pearl over for him. In a sense, what I'm doing will indirectly make Pearl fall in love with Benny. But again, Benny is one of those animals who can't handle the whole truth.

I pass the tractor and scarecrow, hop the fence, and enter the forest. I go towards the teenage boys' campsite. I figure those boys are gonna keep hunting that Ninja Coon until they catch it. At least I now know the mountain lion isn't real.

By the time I reach the teenage boys' camp, their campfires have died down, and they're resting in their tents. Their dog, Dan, is on a leash tied to a nearby tree. I remain downwind of Dan, high up in a tree so he doesn't know I'm around. Despite my precautions, I still have a feeling that somebody is watching me. Perhaps that's just how it feels to lie to everybody. I also feel like I've betrayed Max, the closest thing to what I could call a friend.

I conserve my energy and doze off slightly, but before too long the boys are preparing to hunt. Each of them has a flashlight and a knife, but the leader has the most coveted weapon. He carries a rifle. If I can get that rifle, I'm sure I can figure out how to defeat Patches. No cat can withstand a shot from a rifle. All in good time. All in good time. First, I need to get the Ninja Coon.

My plan is simple. I will stay high in the trees and follow the hunt. If they catch the Ninja Coon, I need to be close so I can somehow snatch away the diamond-studded collar. But what I hope to happen is that I'll follow the hunt, and then when the Ninja Coon hides in his impenetrable lair, I will trap him and take the collar.

The hunt starts. To my surprise, the boys send Dan upstream, away from the haunted barn. The boys follow Dan upstream.

Once they're gone, I inspect their campsite. Food is packed away because of wild animals, but one item of interest remains. A lighter for the campfire rests on a log. I snatch it and place it in a hiding place up in a tree. I'll come back for it later.

I start following the hunt.

After a few minutes, we come to the edge of the forest and a farm that, I think, is Uncle Bill's neighbor. The farm appears abandoned. The house and barn look empty. I make a note to myself that this could be something to ask Patches about.

A broken down and rusty car rests on blocks next to the abandoned barn. Weeds grow tall around it.

Before I get too deeply entangled in my thoughts, D
barks in the distance. He must have caught the scent of the Ninja Coon, and I, even as a spectator for now, feel the thrill of the hunt. Even if the prey can't fight back against a gun, somehow it still feels like an exciting sport.

"Go get him, Dan!" the boys cry out as they chase after Dan. Our route traces a semi-circle so that now we head back in the direction of the teenage boys' campsite. It's tough going, but I manage to stay at the treetops, going from branch to branch to follow the hunt.

We pass the teenage boys' campsite and arrive at a bend in the stream. Dan sniffs around at the bank. That must be how the old Ninja Coon does it: he crosses and floats down the stream so that Dan loses his scent. I'll bet sometimes he goes to the stream and then doubles back to lose Dan. There is no way a dog could understand such tricks. As much as I hate to admit it, raccoons might be one of the few animals as cunning as a cat.

I have to cross the stream, but I can't stay in the treetops. I'll have to go down to the ground and find a way across. If that's the case, I will risk running into those teenage boys, and I know they would love to take a shot at me with their rifle.

Just as I inch my way to the lowest branch of the tree, Dan barks. Instead of crossing the stream, he turns back and runs into the woods. The old Ninja Coon did double back. Dan bolts through the woods with such eagerness, I have a tough time keeping up with the hunt. I lose all caution, not caring whether I'm upwind or downwind of Dan. We're getting close to the Ninja Coon's secret lair.

up, an .s later, we come to a small clearing. The . this clearing is to allow power lines to er. The clearing is empty, save one grand for some reason, was allowed to stand. This is exactly w Patches described the Ninja Coon's secret lair.

Patches told me that one of the unused poles is hollow, and the Ninja Coon walks on a power line that passes over the hollow pole, and then he drops into the hollow to hide. From the ground, the telephone poles appear solid, so you don't think it would be possible for a raccoon to hide inside. As I look at the poles, I already have a guess as to which one is hollow and is concealing the Ninja Coon.

Dan sniffs around the clearing, knowing that the Ninja Coon is nearby, but he can't pinpoint him. I roll my eyes, tired of waiting for this foolish dog to find the old raccoon. It isn't long before the teenage boys show up, and they don't like waiting either.

"Come on, Dan. Where'd he go?" the lead teenage boy asks Dan. Dan whimpers as he sniffs, losing confidence. He starts to sniff around the edges of the forest.

"Come *on*, Dan. We gotta go back into the woods again? You've lost him. Again."

I know they're wrong, though. The boys try to shove Dan into the forest, but he refuses to go. My paws ache as I sit like a statue in the tree, waiting until they leave so I can get that old Ninja Coon when he sneaks out of his secret lair.

I'm not sure if I doze off as I wait, but I snap to my senses when I feel that somebody is watching me. I look around. Perhaps it was an owl? The teenage boys' voices have faded into the forest since they left.

Oh, mouse poop! Did the Ninja Coon already come out of his lair while I dozed?

No way. Dan is just now leaving the clearing. The Ninja Coon won't come out of his hiding place until he is certain that old Dan and the teenage boys are far away. I have to wait just a little more. The diamond-studded collar is within grasp.

***

I smirk as I ponder the giant raccoon hiding at the bottom of the hollowed-out pole. He's lived so long because he's careful. He will wait as long as necessary to be certain it is safe to come out. What he doesn't know is that I am more patient and cunning than him. I would win any stubbornness contest.

My plan is to hide in the oak tree until the Ninja Coon comes out and crawls along the power line back to the oak tree. Once he's in the oak tree, I have the element of surprise. I'll snatch the diamond-studded collar off his tail. Then, I'll push him out of the tree. He'll fall and be stunned as I escape. If not, all I need is that diamond-studded collar. Like I told Patches, it is the key to Pearl's heart. And Pearl is the key to Aunt Susie's and Benny's heart.

I can't gauge how much time passes. I look around the forest, but nothing is happening. Absolutely nothing. Bugs make a few chirps and buzzes, but there are no other animals, and the teenage boys and Dan must be at their campsite sleeping.

But I still feel like somebody is watching me. I look all around me as best I can without moving a single muscle, just in case the Ninja Coon comes up out of the telephone pole. I rotate my ears as much as I can. My eyes, ears, and nose tell me nobody is watching me. It's just me in this tree, and the Ninja Coon in the hollowed-out pole. But I just can't shake the feeling that somebody is watching.

Where's a giant rainstorm when I need one?

If the pole started filling up with water, I guarantee the Ninja Coon would come out.

As I ponder this, I no longer have the feeling that I'm being watched, but now I do smell something. It is something I've never smelled before. Before I can place what it is, it's gone. I'm no hunting dog like Dan. My sense of smell is not nearly as good as his. It somehow reminds me when I first entered the haunted barn, and I couldn't quite place the scent of Patches. This is a different scent, but I don't know what it is.

But it's gone now.

I'm fed up with this old Ninja Coon. I could walk along the wire myself to the hollow pole, and look down in there. That would scare the Ninja Coon out for sure. Even if he comes out in the most ferocious manner, I'll have the high ground. I would have plenty of time to maneuver myself in a position to grab the diamond-studded collar when he comes out.

If the Ninja Coon could get on and walk along the power line without being electrocuted, it must not be live.

I put my front paws on the power cable, and I look ahead.

This will be some tight wire act. I've never walked on anything this thin. Even for a cat of my caliber, this is a challenge. Good thing the fate of the world doesn't depend on Max doing this.

I hope Max is okay.

That will help me focus. I'm doing this for Max. Patches thinks it's for him, but it's ultimately for Max. I imagine Max standing on top of the hollowed-out pole, and I put one paw in front of the other towards Max. I make a few cautious steps along the power line. It is taut and sturdy. It definitely won't be moving.

I move faster along the power cable.

I reach the halfway point.

ROAR!

A sharp roar rips through the air and almost knocks me off the cable. I hang by my front paws.

Instinctively, I swing my hind legs up and get back on.

I look around the woods, startled. It's silent again. I don't see anything. I don't care if the mountain lion is only Patches' troops. Were they trying to scare somebody else away? I guess Patches' troops were the ones watching me.

Just a few more steps…

I hop off the power cable and onto the pole. I peer down into the hollowed-out pole. I expect to see the Ninja Coon glaring up at me, baring his ugly yellow fangs.

But I see absolutely nothing.

What the litter box?

There is no Ninja Coon in there. Absolutely nothing.

That old Ninja Coon must have continued along the power line and never stopped inside this hollowed-out pole. If so, who knows where he's gone since then? There's no chance of me catching the Ninja Coon and the diamond-studded collar tonight.

I'll have to get the Ninja Coon tomorrow night. Before then, I'll have some explaining to do to both Patches and Uncle Bill's farm animals.

CHAPTER 8

As I make my way back to the farm, I collect the lighter I hid in a tree. The early morning sun warms the forest. Now is the only time of day it's cool and light at the same time. Moos emanate from the cow pasture as I approach the farm. I've been turning over in my head all the options I have now that I failed to catch the Ninja Coon. I hope I have another chance to capture the Ninja Coon tomorrow night before Patches intervenes. If Patches' troops were watching me last night, he knows I didn't get the Ninja Coon or the diamond-studded collar.

"Halt! Who goes there?" Benny calls out as I approach the fence on the edge of Uncle Bill's farm.

"It's me," I call back. "Good job as a guard dog, but you don't have to worry about me."

Benny emerges from behind a fence post.

"Did you see her?" Benny asks. "Did you talk to her? Is Pearl falling in love with me?"

"I haven't had a chance to talk with Pearl. I need the diamond-studded collar. Don't you worry. I'll get it tonight, and then you'll have the key to Pearl's heart."

"What happened last night? I thought—"

"Something important came up," I lie to Benny. "It was Max. You know how he's not so bright, and so I need to watch out for him, especially in this forest. He is having a great time playing with all those bugs and… stuff he's finding in the woods." My lie is precariously thin, but I can only hope Benny is blinded by his love for Pearl. It's also a reminder that I will have to explain to everybody where Max is. If I don't come up with something good, the rest of the animals will brand me a traitor.

"What do you think you're doing?" Elmer calls out as he runs towards me and Benny. "Benny, you are supposed to raise the alarm when anybody approaches. And I mean *anybody*." Elmer looks at me with squinted eyes and says, "Where is Max?"

There is no way I can tell the truth now, and so I call upon the one positive thing I know about these farm animals.

"You won't believe it," I say with a smile, "but it will be the best news you have heard in a long time."

"Did you find matching diamond earrings for Pearl?" Benny asks.

"Is there a sheep herding contest nearby?" Elmer asks.

Farm animals: always thinking about themselves.

"Oh, it's so good," I promise, "that we should gather everybody in the barn so I can tell all of you."

Elmer thinks for a few seconds.

"It better be good," Elmer says as he turns back to Uncle Bill's barn. Benny and I follow.

Benny asks me along the way, "So what is it? You can tell me, your buddy, before everybody else, right?"

I need as much goodwill as I can muster, but I haven't figured out what to say yet. I only have an inkling of an idea.

I mouth the name, "Alfie."

Benny gives me a confused look.

"Alfie?" Benny mouths back so that Elmer doesn't hear. Benny is not an expert lip reader.

"Just wait," I whisper.

Once we're in the barn, Elmer addresses all the farm animals.

"Princess has some good news to tell us," Elmer announces. "As you can see, Max is not with her, but she has promised we will all want to hear this."

"The good news I bring," I say, "is about your beloved Alfie."

Everybody falls silent except for a few gasps of, "Alfie?"

"What a shocking discovery!" Ned the interviewing horse says. "All of our viewers are dying for more."

"All of you know about the farm next door," I say. "It is abandoned, except for Alfie."

"What is Alfie doing there?" Ned the interviewing horse asks.

"Alfie started his own retreat center for self improvement."

"What is that?" Elmer asks before Ned.

"You all know what that is," I say. I begin to draw on things I've heard while I was laying on top of the TV at home. "For example: Elmer, you are a pig, but you want to shepherd sheep. If I understand you right, Alfie encouraged you to pursue your dream, and so you've become the best shepherding pig there is. You have followed your own dreams to become what you want."

Elmer smiles, proud of himself. Playing on his pride seems to work.

"And you, Ned," I say to the horse, "you dream of being an interviewer on TV. You're pursuing your dream, too."

"Alfie was an exceptional leader," I continue. "But he wanted to help more than just you. He wanted to help many animals. The best way to do that was to set up a training center for many animals. Alfie teaches them to pursue their dreams."

This starts to sound so good, I'm beginning to believe myself.

"Well I'm quite excited for Alfie," Betsy the sheep says. The rest of the farm animals voice their agreement.

"Let's go see him," Benny says to the whole group.

"There's more I need to tell you," I say. "You can't go see him right now." Everybody stares at me with questioning eyes. They desperately want to see Alfie.

"Max is with Alfie right now." I continue the lie. "You all noticed that Max is not the smartest cat in the world."

"I did see him lick a fencepost," David the vegan goat says, "and not even a goat would eat a fencepost."

"I saw him chase his own tail," Benny says, "and that's something only goofy dogs do."

"Believe me," I say, "that's not the least of it. So Max is now with Alfie at Alfie's training center next door. They cannot be disturbed. Max desperately needs Alfie's help. You know how good Alfie was for you. You know how much Alfie helped you. But if he's going to help Max, he needs several more days undisturbed to finish the training."

"All right then," Elmer calls out, "a few more days, and then we will see Alfie, and Max will be a new cat. I'm sorry we ever doubted you, Princess."

Elmer beams at me, having believed my lies completely.

I've bought myself more time, but now I have to figure out how to get Max back and explain that Alfie is not next door. Before I forget, I hide the stolen lighter near my sleeping spot in the barn. I comfort myself with the fact that these farm animals won't harm me like Patches will if I don't find a way out of this mess.

***

As I follow Dan's hunt for the Ninja Coon the next night, I feel like I'm getting the hang of it. Dan is so focused on the Ninja Coon, he doesn't notice me following in the treetops. I need to stay close in case Dan catches the Ninja Coon so that I can snatch the diamond-studded collar.

The chase winds away from the teenagers' camp, and we pass the deserted farm where Alfie is supposedly training Max. The Ninja Coon is making his way to his lair.

This is almost too easy.

That's what I think until the Ninja Coon decides to cross the stream. Dan needs to be careful that the Ninja Coon doesn't simply float downstream. Or, he might pretend he's going to cross the stream but then double back like he did before. It seems that this time, though, the Ninja Coon really did cross the stream.

Dan checks along the shore to make sure the Ninja Coon isn't playing tricks on him. He then gaily fords the stream while barking, eager to sink his fangs into that big coon.

This is the only part of the hunt I'm afraid of. I can't follow in the treetops. I need to descend down to the ground and cross the stream. The Ninja Coon will need to cross back to his lair. But what if Dan catches the Ninja Coon first? I can't risk that. I need to find a way across the stream before those rifle-toting teenage boys catch up.

"Go get him, Dan!" the boys call out.

I shuttle down the tree and run to a large group of boulders which reaches out into the stream. Surely I'll find a way across on these rocks. I leap boulder to boulder to cross.

Before I reach the halfway point, I can't go any farther. I backtrack a few rocks, and then I work my way up onto a large rock so that I can see the best route forward. I spot a better route, and I hurry down the backside of the large rock. I turn to make my way along the new route.

When I'm about halfway across the stream, Dan charges out of the woods directly at me. He bares his teeth and growls at me.

I dash back the way I came, and I leap onto a large rock. Dan splashes into the stream, and he looks up at me.

"You've become overconfident, cat," Dan says. "I smelled you the other night. You've gotten too close to the hunt this time. Leave my master's forest. Otherwise, my master will shoot you with his rifle."

"I praise you, oh masterful hunting hound," I say to flatter Dan. "Your loyalty is admirable. You serve him well." This is difficult to say because I know how horrible Dan's master is. "Your master will indeed arrive soon with his rifle, but tell me why your master is so worthy of your loyalty?"

"I don't have time for this," Dan says. "He's my master. That's all there is."

"That's not all there is."

Dan blinks, eager to hear the rest of the story.

"I was there two nights ago during the heavy rain storm," I say. "Your master deserted you when he hurried back to his tent to escape the rain. He said things to demean you." This isn't true; he had said Dan was "fine." I'm sick of lying to everybody, but I guess that's what happens when one chooses the path of the snake.

"You lie," Dan says. "My master is as loyal to me as I am to him. Besides, I can handle this raccoon on my own."

"It didn't seem that way when I had to scare him off your drowning head," I say.

Dan can't hide his surprise.

"That's right," I press on. "I was there when you almost drowned in the stream as the raccoon used you as a raft. Your master wasn't there to save you. He abandoned you." Dan furrows his brow and shakes his head. "I saved your life, Dan," I lie. "I scared him off of your head so that you could escape drowning."

In reality, Patches' troops acting as a mountain lion scared the Ninja Coon away. What matters for now, though, is that Dan thinks I saved his life.

"Dan! Where are you? Go get him!" the now much closer teenage boy yells. He'll be here in seconds.

"I don't trust you," Dan says, "but there's no other way you could know about the raccoon nearly drowning me. I am a dog of honor. I owe you a life debt. I'll do what I can to help you, as long as it doesn't harm my master."

"My only interest in the raccoon," I say, "is the diamond-studded collar on its tail. When you catch it, make sure that you get that diamond-studded collar for me."

Dan nods in agreement.

"Hey," the teenage boy yells, close enough to see us, "that's no coon! Get going, Dan!"

The lead boy aims his rifle at me, and I dash across the stream on rocks.

Crack!

A rifle shot rings out, but the bullet ricochets off a rock into a nearby tree. I climb a tree to follow Dan on the hunt.

Just as I reach the top branches, Dan comes running back. My heart sinks.

Has he lost the scent of the Ninja Coon?

I follow Dan on the hunt. It's much easier now that I don't have to worry about Dan noticing me. I think my presence motivates Dan. He performs not only for his master, but also for a cat.

Unfortunately, Dan doesn't have a chance to impress me. As dawn approaches, Dan still hasn't trapped the Ninja Coon. The teenage boys call off the hunt, and I follow them back to their campsite.

Dan must be mad at me. It was because of our confrontation that the Ninja Coon got away.

How will I explain my failure to Patches?

***

"It doesn't hurt them, does it?" the youngest girl child asks Uncle Bill as they enter the barn with the oldest girl child and a large sack. I'm resting during the day, exhausted from my nighttime adventures. The boy child is not with them. I wonder where he could be.

"You gotta do it now and then," Uncle Bill informs the children. "It will be good fun for you to watch me shear Gus and Betsy the sheep. They don't like it before and during, but they sure are glad after they get their wool sheared off. It's a lot cooler for them."

This ought to be amusing.

The old tractor roars to life in the pasture. Uncle Bill must have given the middle boy child permission to drive the tractor.

"Breaking news!" Ned announces. "Gus and Betsy are going to get their wool sheared off. Everybody gather around!"

"You all heard Ned," Elmer instructs the farm animals. "Everybody gather around. This sure will be fun."

"Except for us!" Gus and Betsy object in unison.

I watch from above in the hayloft, and all the other animals gather around Gus and Betsy's pen. Uncle Bill pulls giant shears out of the sack.

"Be careful, Uncle Bill," the youngest girl child says.

"Go for it, Uncle Bill," the oldest girl child says, urging Uncle Bill on.

Uncle Bill crouches in a wide stance. He inches towards Gus and Betsy, backing them into a corner. Uncle Bill lunges forward, but he grasps at air as the sheep break in opposite directions.

"I'll get the biggest one first," Uncle Bill says. That means Gus.

Uncle Bill resumes his wide stance. Betsy dashes away, but Uncle Bill ignores her. He inches closer to Gus, whose eyes dart about, seeking an escape.

Uncle Bill moves to wrap his arm around Gus' neck, but just as he does, Betsy butts him in the behind with her head. Uncle Bill falls face first into the manure pile, futilely grasping for Gus as he falls. This brings a chorus of cheers and *ewwww* from us spectators.

Uncle Bill curses under his breath, but he catches himself and smiles for the children.

"It's all part of the fun," Uncle Bill says, forcing another grin.

The youngest girl child covers her eyes, afraid to watch. The oldest girl child, however, has a smile that stretches from ear to ear. Even the boy child would be enjoying this, but I still hear the tractor running outside.

Gus breathes heavily, tired from running and dodging. Gus can't move as fast now that he's tired, and Betsy is probably afraid to knock over the farmer that feeds her. Uncle Bill lunges and wraps his arms around Gus. Uncle Bill holds Gus down with one arm as he turns on the shears in his other hand.

Buzzzzz. The shears hum in Uncle Bill's hand. He runs the clippers over Gus, and white wool falls in bunches to the ground.

The farm animals whoop, holler, and laugh at Gus's public embarrassment. He looks hilarious. It appears he has lost half his body weight. The shearing has revealed a naked and pinkish body. Gus hides in the corner after Uncle Bill releases him.

"Be quiet," he tells the crowd. "It's not funny. It's just part of nature."

"He's right," Elmer says to the farm animals. But even Elmer can hardly contain his laughter as he looks at Gus.

Uncle Bill catches Betsy after a few attempts. He's about to assault her wool with the shears.

The barn shakes with a crash, and Betsy escapes.

Daylight streams through the opposite wall of the barn.

The tractor engine roars nearby.

The tractor has crashed into the barn, breaking through the wall. The front half of the tractor is now inside the barn.

The farm animals run around in shock. Uncle Bill gets up, forgetting about Betsy, and rushes to the two girl children.

Boom!

The tractor backfires as it idles amid the debris, sending the animals into even more of a frenzy.

"Are you two okay?" Uncle Bill asks the girls, pulling them close to him.

"What happened?" the oldest girl child asks.

"I'm okay, but scared," the youngest girl child says.

The middle boy child turns off the tractor and stumbles to the ground, dazed.

Uncle Bill runs over to him.

"Are you okay?" Uncle Bill asks.

The middle boy child walks like a zombie, but he doesn't appear physically hurt.

"It wouldn't stop, it wouldn't stop," the middle boy child mutters to Uncle Bill.

Uncle Bill shoos the animals back into their pens. He sends the children back to the people's house. He stays behind to examine the damage. He is soon satisfied the barn is structurally safe.

Uncle Bill starts the tractor and inches it back out of the hole it created. He cuts the engine, gets down, and inspects the mechanics of the tractor.

He scratches his head.

Uncle Bill enters the barn and looks at all of us animals in turn. I don't know what he's thinking, but he's suspicious.

"None of you would have, or could have, chewed up the brake wires. The teeth look too big even for rat..." Uncle Bill continues, thinking out loud.

Oh no.

Somebody sabotaged the tractor so that it would crash. I don't know if was Patches, the Ninja Coon, or both. I bet one of them sabotaged the tractor in hopes of killing Uncle Bill. This needs to end soon, and if this is going to end soon, I must catch the Ninja Coon tonight and get that diamond-studded collar.

Elmer goes up to Uncle Bill and rubs against his leg.

"Hey there, Elmer boy," Uncle Bill says with a sigh. "It's not the end of the world. But it sure got me worried. Somebody could have been hurt. Or worse. I'll stack some hay bales in the hole until I have time to repair the wall before winter. Oh well. I guess I can look forward to hiking and camping in the woods."

Uncle Bill trudges back to his house.

I need that diamond-studded collar. I'm afraid Patches will attempt to kill Uncle Bill when he's hiking and camping in the woods, especially if they go near the haunted barn.

CHAPTER 9

"Do we *have* to go?" the middle boy child asks. Uncle Bill, the big man person, and the three children hike with camping gear past the scarecrow and towards the forest. I sneak along.

"A short hike will do you good," the big man person says.

"There's nothing more fun than cooking dinner over a campfire and then sleeping in a tent," Uncle Bill says.

"We're not going near that haunted barn, are we?" asks the youngest girl child.

"Not even close," Uncle Bill reassures her.

Benny races after them as they reach the edge of the forest.

"Don't go! Don't go!" Benny barks at them.

Of course, they don't understand, so Uncle Bill says, "Why don't you come with us, Benny?"

Benny looks back to the barn, aware that Elmer forbid any of us from going into the forest. After a second, Benny rushes headlong into the forest with the people.

The sun will be setting in about an hour, and so I decide it's best that I join them. I follow above, in the forest's canopy. Nobody knows I'm there. People move more slowly than Dan on the hunt, so this is easy.

We head between the old haunted barn and the teenagers' campsite. We cross the stream and push deeper into the woods. Several minutes later, the kids complain about how heavy their packs are and how they are sick and tired of hiking.

"We'll set up camp in the next clearing," Uncle Bill says. "Dusk will come soon, anyways."

Minutes later, we enter a clearing in the woods, and all three of the children plop their packs down and grumble about their grueling hike, even though it couldn't have been more than an hour long.

"I'll get the fire started while you kids gather sticks and logs," the big man person says. Uncle Bill sets up the tents.

"I'll start the fire," the boy child says.

"Get wood first, and then you can help," the big man person counters. The boy child heads into the woods with slumped shoulders, searching for sticks and branches. His sisters follow.

Not much later, the fire roars, and Uncle Bill explains they will cook dinner once the fire dies down to coals. It's not yet completely dark, but without the fire, the people would not be able to see.

Just then I hear a noise I don't like. It's those raucous teenage boys, coming towards our campsite.

"Who's there?" the lead teenage boy calls out.

"It's me. Bill. You best not cause any trouble. I own these woods, remember?"

The teenage boy steps into the circle of light cast by the slowly dying fire. His buddies stand behind him. He holds his rifle across his chest.

"We will be hunting coons tonight," the lead teenage boy says. "So you better be careful. It would be a shame if any of you were accidentally shot."

"I don't care who your dad is," Uncle Bill barks at the teenage boy. I've never heard Uncle Bill speak so harshly. "These woods are mine, and they're gonna stay mine. As a matter of fact, I forbid you from hunting on my property."

"I'm only trying to help you," the teenage boy says sarcastically. "You need to keep the raccoon population down. And don't you young ones forget," the teenage boy says as he leans in and then whispers, "don't forget about the mountain lion and the haunted barn."

His warning hangs in the air, and the children stare with fear. The middle boy child's eyes fix on the rifle. Uncle Bill glares defiantly. Before he can say anything, the teenager continues.

"I don't care if you forbid me to hunt tonight. My dad will own this whole forest soon and turn it into condominiums. What are you gonna do to stop me?"

The teenage boy turns around and leads his buddies into the dark forest. Uncle Bill doesn't respond to his defiance.

"That teenage boy is too big for his britches," Uncle Bill says once they are gone. "I don't care who his dad is. Nothing his dad does will get my farm and forest out of my hands and into his so he can turn it into a big and fancy condo association."

"The fire is about ready," my big man person says. "Let's fry up some bacon." The mention of bacon lightens the mood.

"Benny will love that," Uncle Bill says. The two adult men look at each other, and then they look around. "Where is Benny?" Uncle Bill asks. The three children shrug their shoulders.

"Benny!" Uncle Bill calls out.

"I'll go look for him," the middle boy child says. "I've gotta go pee, anyways." He gets up and walks the same way the teenage boys left.

I race down the tree and go straight towards the abandoned farm. I sneak past the middle boy child, who hasn't stopped to go pee yet. When I think I'm about two-thirds of the way to the abandoned barn, I see Benny coming towards me. He trots along slowly with his head down. He doesn't see me because he's so dejected.

"Benny," I say when I get close. "Where have you been?"

"You've been lying this whole time," Benny says with defiance. He's not only dejected, but also angry. "I need to warn the others about your lies, and there's nothing you can do about it. You haven't gotten any diamond-studded collar. And there's nobody at that farm next door. Certainly not Alfie or Max. What really happened to Max? Were you somehow involved with Alfie's disappearance, too? You've been lying to us this whole time because you just want to take over Uncle Bill's farm."

"There's more going on than you realize. I'm trying to do what's best for Uncle Bill and his farm. There's a real enemy out there, but I'm about to turn the tables on him." I wince as I tell another lie.

"You don't get another chance," Benny says. "I'm going back to Uncle Bill's farm, and I'm gonna tell Elmer the truth."

Benny pushes past me. Instead of heading back towards the campsite, he heads towards Uncle Bill's farm.

I go after him to convince him not to tell Elmer and the other farm animals, but then a loud howl splits the air. It's Dan, signaling the beginning of the hunt.

"Trust me just one more night," I call out after Benny. He shakes his head as he continues.

I have no choice but to leave Benny and join the hunt with Dan for the Ninja Coon.

***

I race towards Dan's barking. Tonight, the hunt unfolds differently.

I no longer have to stay up in the trees away from Dan. This makes it easier to follow the Ninja Coon across the stream. I just have to be sure the teenage boys with the rifle don't see me.

The chase takes us in one giant loop. After about twenty or thirty minutes (it's hard to tell), we're back where the hunt started. We've gone near the Ninja Coon's lair, deep into the woods, back towards the old haunted barn, away from the haunted barn, and back towards the Ninja Coon's lair. We cross the stream multiple times, but Dan stays on the trail.

Even I, an excellent physical specimen, grow tired after two large loops. Dan continues the hunt with dogged energy, but I fear he may not have the patience that comes with age and wisdom.

During the third loop, I realize what the old Ninja Coon's strategy may be. He wants to make Dan careless. So far, Dan has been able to stay on the track easily. After doing the same route many times, I bet the Ninja Coon is going to give Dan the slip.

The teenage boys whoop and holler during the hunt, but it weakens as the hunt stretches through the night. That's part of the Ninja Coon's tactic: make everybody bored with the hunt so they either make a mistake or quit.

At one of the stream crossings, Dan boldly splashes across the stream. Dan plunges headlong into the woods on the opposite bank. I start to follow, but Dan doesn't howl.

Dan has lost the trail. I was right; that old Ninja Coon lulled Dan to sleep by repeatedly going the same route, and now he's tricked him. Dan hurries past me, saliva dripping out his jowls.

"He doubled back! He doubled back!" Dan gasps.

I follow Dan back across the stream. Dan takes a few minutes to pick up the scent before we continue. My hope dissipates like food in my food bowl because I know the Ninja Coon has gained important time.

The hunt now winds towards the Ninja Coon's lair. This raises my hopes. He can't hide in that hollowed out pole, and he's not going to escape on the power line that continues into the forest. I'll have him trapped. I will soon grasp victory with my paw.

My ears perk up as we draw closer to the lair in the clearing. I notice something. Something is not right. The teenage boys have gone quiet.

But just as Dan reaches the clearing—

ROAR!

The roar of a mountain lion breaks through the night. Dan yelps, turns back towards me, and retreats with his tail between his legs.

As he rushes past, I urge him, "Go back, go back! It's not really a mountain lion! It's..."

It's no use. Dan won't listen. I can't convince him it's really just a bunch of well-coordinated cats and not a mountain lion.

The forest clearing is deathly quiet. The Ninja Coon is quiet, wherever he is. There's not even a breeze rustling the oak tree leaves. The air sits still, warm, and somehow electric. I step into the clearing, look towards the solitary oak tree, and just as I do, a massive thunderstorm ensues.

Twin bolts of lightning streak through the sky, illuminating the clearing like day for a second. The thunderclap immediately follows. I cower from the sheer volume of this force of nature that threatens to break my eardrums. Then the heavy raindrops commence their bombardment.

I won't allow a thunderstorm to save the Ninja Coon.

I rush towards the oak tree to climb up to the power line. As I approach the tree, another cat slinks down it. Once I'm under the branches where the rain can't touch me, I encounter Patches. The diamond-studded collar sparkles in his mouth. He flicks it to my feet.

"I am deeply disappointed in your failure, Princess," Patches says. Three more of Patches' troops come down from the oak tree, and more enter the clearing from the edges of the forest.

Right now, I'm not worried about Patches.

I see Max amongst his troops. I barely recognize him at first, but one of the troops is mostly orange except for his white feet and a spot on his back. Fur is missing in areas, he has several scratches, he is muscular, but he is definitely Max.

Can I really call him Max if he's no longer that silly, playful kitten?

***

Max?

The cat doesn't respond.

I'm not sure if I said it aloud.

"How are you doing? How have you been?" I ask as I take a few steps towards Max. I can't hide the concern in my voice. This might be the first time I've been concerned for somebody other than myself.

"This is the cat you used to call Max," Patches says, stepping in between us. "He won't respond to that name anymore. He has a new identity within the New Order."

What has Max gone through in re-education?

"Call him Trainee 44. He is the forty-fourth to join my New Order."

"You have forty-four cats in the old haunted barn?" I ask.

"Not at all," Patches says. "Many trainees don't survive. A radical transformation of mind and body is required. Changing from a feeble house cat, who only pretends to be the master, into a warrior who can truly dominate is difficult. Honestly, I expected Max to die. Cats with greater promise have."

Patches comes closer to me and looks me in the eyes.

"I don't sense disapproval from you, do I?" Patches asks.

"Of course not," I say. I must pretend to work with Patches for his silly New Order. "It is genius, and it surprises me."

Genius, and yet monstrous.

"Those weak farm animals on Uncle Bill's farm have told you about Alfie?" Patches asks.

"Not much," I say, hoping Patches will give me useful information.

"I had hoped Alfie would join my New Order, but he resisted. He couldn't survive."

The thunderstorm is over. I look again directly into Max's eyes, but I fear that he may be lost. He may truly be Trainee 44, and not Max. My mind swirls as I realize that, just a few weeks ago, I would've been thrilled to be rid of Max. Now that he's Trainee 44, I can't stand it. I want to win him back.

A moth flutters above Max's head, floats down, and lands on Max's nose. A week ago, Max would have played with it for the next twenty minutes. Tonight, he twitches his nose, and the moth flutters away. If any of the real Max remains inside the warrior shell, it would have shown then.

Shouts from teenage boys nearby in the forest divert my attention. It sounds like the teenage boys are fighting.

"You thief!" the lead teenage boy yells while the others yell insults.

I can't discern what else the teenage boys say, but the tone tells me one of the boys is defending himself.

"You're going to get what you deserve!" I hear from the teenage boys.

What follows sounds like a fistfight. I can't imagine what fighting is like without claws and fangs. I look over to Patches, and he grins.

"This is good," he says to me. He seems to think I'm on his side.

The fighting amongst the teenage boys lasts less than a minute. Before it's over, a few more troops come out of the woods. Two of them drag something behind them.

Those cats stole the rifle from the teenage boy.

I piece it together: Patches' troops stole the rifle from the teenage boy, and somebody has to bear the blame. That's why they were fighting. But who would the boys distrust in their own group so much to beat him up?

Oh, no.

It must be the middle boy child whom they think stole the rifle. He had snuck away, claiming to need the bathroom.

"I do hope you are able to break those sentimental connections with your people," Patches says. "My troops informed me that the boy child got in a fight with those other teenage boys. No matter, though. I need this rifle more than those boys do. Besides, there's no more Ninja Coon to hunt."

"That foolish boy child deserves whatever he got," I say to Patches. This lie makes me sick like a hairball, but I need to maintain this charade if I'm going to turn on Patches at a key point.

"Take this diamond-studded collar with you. Carry out your plan for my purposes. I do hope that even though you were not competent to defeat the Ninja Coon, you will use it to get Uncle Bill into his barn tomorrow night."

"I need to get Uncle Bill into his barn tomorrow night?" I ask to clarify.

"It's simple. You can do it, can't you?" Patches asks as he stares at me. He's testing me, I know. "If not, I'm sure Trainee 44 could handle it."

"I can handle it," I say.

"Good," Patches says as a smile grows on his face. "I will be there with the rifle to shoot him. Since this rifle belongs to the developer's son, and the developer wants Uncle Bill's farm, the developer will be blamed for the murder. Uncle Bill won't be around anymore. Aunt Susie will leave because of hard memories, but the developer won't be able to take over the farm. I will then take over the farm with ease."

"Ingenious," I say to flatter Patches.

It's a despicable plan.

"For your part," Patches says, "make sure Uncle Bill is in his barn tomorrow night."

With one last look at Max, I snatch up the diamond-studded collar and race back to Uncle Bill's farm.

CHAPTER 10

As I run back to Uncle Bill's farm with the diamond-studded collar in my mouth, the morning dew is glistens, and I struggle to think of a way to turn on Patches and defeat him.

Max is no longer the silly playful kitten I despised.

He transformed into Patches' twisted version of what it means to be a cat.

I don't have any allies. Benny discovered that the neighbor's farm sits empty. Everybody will know I lied about Max and Alfie. Unless I can stretch the lie more, and claim that...

But I can't stretch that lie any further. Before I think of a coherent way to get the farm animals to help me defeat Patches, anger wells up in my chest. It clouds my vision and strategy.

I reach the edge of the forest, and I wait outside the fence of Uncle Bill's farm. The scarecrow stares at me.

Everything seems normal from here, but I know that things are radically different. The animals in the barn will want to be rid of me. None of them know about Patches.

My children people, the big man person, and Uncle Bill are still camping in the woods. They'll wake up later this morning and come home, I suppose. The middle boy child got beat up. I wonder if he cried himself to sleep in his tent, or if he stumbled back to his mother here on Uncle Bill's farm. No matter. The only chance I have is with this diamond-studded collar. If I win Pearl over to Benny with it, then Benny will help me.

That's what I hope, anyways.

I cross the fence and head to Uncle Bill's house. I must avoid the farm animals until I've won Pearl and then Benny to my side through this diamond-studded collar. I enter Uncle Bill's house through the doggy door. The house is completely quiet. I don't bother to climb up into the rafters and rush instead to Pearl's back room. She snuggles up on custom suede sleeping pad. Of course, my people have a queen-sized bed for me, but I guess a fancy cushion on the floor isn't bad for a dog.

"Pearl," I say as loudly as I dare. "Pearl," I say, a little louder.

"I'm sorry, I'm sorry, I can't give autographs now," Pearl says without opening her eyes. She must be dreaming.

I nudge Pearl gently.

It's time for me to speak her language.

"Your beauty is so blinding, you don't need beauty sleep," I say. "Besides, I have a gift for you."

Pearl opens groggy eyes and looks at me with a confused expression.

"What are you doing here?" Pearl asks. "Did my bodyguard let you in?"

I decide not to inform her that she doesn't have a bodyguard.

"Look at this beautiful diamond-studded collar," I say. "Benny got it for you. Did you hear me? Benny got it for you. Don't you love Benny?" This last part is pushy, but I can't wait for love to work its magic slowly. This needs to happen fast.

Pearl stretches and grits her teeth to wake up. As she stretches, I see something glisten on her neck. She's wearing a new diamond-studded collar.

"That old thing?" Pearl says with a glance at the collar I offered. "That was stylish, like, about a month ago. Susie got me the latest in canine accessories. I can't count how many carats are around my neck now."

Pearl strikes a few poses so that I can see her new diamond-studded collar from several angles.

"Impressive," I say. "The diamonds are much larger and better than your old collar."

"I know," Pearl says, "it's almost a blessing I lost the old collar. Otherwise, Susie wouldn't have gotten me this new one."

"All the same," I say, "Benny performed magnificently heroic feats to win back this diamond-studded collar for you."

"That overgrown hot dog is silly," Pearl says. "The type of man I want to marry would have known that I need the latest diamond-studded collar. I am Pearl, after all." Pearl lifts her nose in the air before she settles down to continue sleeping.

This is bad news. Now I really do have no allies. If I had known that this diamond-studded collar wasn't going to do any good, I would not have spent three nights running through the forest after a mangy old raccoon, risking my life amongst hunting dogs and rifles. I can't waste more time here.

I rush out of the house without saying anything else. I need a plan before I face Elmer and the farm animals.

I go away from the barn, towards the cow-tipping pasture. It's just a minute or two away, and the cows don't seem to remember me. Some of them munch on grass, but most of them are sleeping. Maybe for one last *hurrah* before I meet my end, I'll try to give one of those cows a good tipping. Sitting here, looking down from a fence, I realize what I'm missing.

I wish Chief was here. Chief lives next door back at my house. He's old, can hardly move, and on most days he doesn't get halfway out of his doghouse. He's lived long enough that he's actually accumulated some wisdom by accident over the years. I hate to admit it, but I wish I could hear his advice now.

***

Chief: what would you say if you were here?

"You sure got yourself dug into a deep hole here," I imagine Chief saying.

"Everything I've done and said is for their own good. They just don't know that it would be best if I was in charge," I say to imaginary Chief.

"Once you think the ends justifies the means, there's bound to be nothing but problems," imaginary Chief says. I'm not sure how I know Chief would say that, but I got a feeling he would.

"But if they would believe me for just a little bit longer, then I'll find a way to make everything turn out all right. I am Princess, after all," I would say.

"What you mean is that if everybody would believe more of your lies. But everything would not turn out okay. You would be in bigger trouble than you are now," imaginary Chief tells me. "Let's suppose everything does turn out okay after all of your lies. How would you feel if your rule over this farm was based on lies?"

"I—"

"How would you feel if another cat was in charge of this farm, but it was only because he lied to and cheated all the farm animals, Uncle Bill, and Aunt Susie?"

"I would expose the lies and get rid of that cat," I say.

"*Hmmmm,*" Chief ponders.

I'm starting to wonder if I accidentally chewed some catnip.

"How will I get those farm animals back on my side against Patches?" I ask imaginary Chief. "I've done wrong, but that doesn't mean Patches should rule."

"Haven't you learned anything about trust?" Chief asks.

This imaginary old dog is getting a little bristly for my liking, but I'm desperate.

"I do remember something you said. 'In order for people to like you, they need to trust you.'"

"Sounds about right to me," imaginary Chief says, "but I'm half deaf and blind. What do I know?"

"But after all my lies…?"

"It only takes a tiny misstep to lose trust, but it takes a long time to gain it back," imaginary Chief says. "The best way is to start with a clean slate."

"I need to admit I lied?"

"And you need to apologize, too," imaginary Chief says.

"I'm Princess—the *empress,*" I object. "How can I rule if I reveal how fallible I am?"

"If you don't, you will only be the empress in title, but you won't have any true authority," imaginary Chief says. "Admit what you did, apologize, and start from there."

I walk away from the cow pasture and imaginary Chief, back towards the barn. Chief is right, but this is the toughest advice I've ever received. I'm not sure how to admit I'm wrong and apologize.

I've never done so in my life.

***

The warm wind blows against my face as I walk to Uncle Bill's barn.

I'm going to come clean.

I'm going to tell the whole truth to set things right. And honestly, it's what I need to do to be in charge.

Before I reach the barn, Elmer comes out. He stands by the entrance, about twenty feet away.

"You've got a lot of nerve coming here," Elmer says.

"I do. But not for the reasons you think."

Benny has at least told Elmer.

"I wouldn't take one more step if I were you," Elmer says.

"Benny told you part of the truth," I say, "but I need to tell you the whole truth."

"From what Benny told me," Elmer says, "nothing you say can change anything."

As I get ready to tell Elmer about Patches, I realize how ridiculous it sounds.

Truth is stranger than fiction, I remember Chief saying.

"My lies aren't the worst of your problems," I say. "It doesn't mean much to you, but my lies were well-intentioned."

Elmer shakes his head in disbelief. My lies were mostly for my selfish good. Gaining a conscience is an uncomfortable thing, I'm discovering.

"My motivation was to save your and Uncle Bill's life," I say. "That is the truth. Let me tell you more of the truth Benny doesn't know."

"Keep your forked tongue behind your teeth," Elmer warns. Elmer scratches his front hoof in the dirt.

"I know who stole the eggs from the chicken coop," I say. "It's the same one who stole the fish when Uncle Bill went fishing. It is the same animal who sabotaged Uncle Bill's tractor in an attempt, I believe, to kill Uncle Bill."

"Who?" Elmer asks. Suspicion comes through his squinted eyes.

"There is, or, there was," I say, correcting myself, "a giant raccoon. He went by the name of the Ninja Coon."

"You lie," Elmer says. "If what you're saying is true, why didn't you tell us sooner?"

"I wanted to save all of you myself—"

"You wanted all the credit for yourself," Elmer says. "Did this mystical Ninja Coon also make Max disappear? Or, let me guess: this Ninja Coon trapped Max in the haunted barn? I know Uncle Bill only tells stories about that old haunted barn to keep kids away."

"This will be difficult for you to believe," I say, "but you need to hear me out. There is an army of warrior cats gathering. I know the leader from when I was much younger, but I didn't know he was gathering an army here until recently. In order to save all of you, including Uncle Bill, I had no choice but to join this army. I planned to cross him, but Max resisted. This cat took Max into his army, and he's done something to Max's brain so that he is now one of his soldiers. This cat's base for his army is in that old haunted barn."

"This is preposterous!" Elmer mutters with disgust.

"I know more. The mountain lion you've heard is not a mountain lion. This cat figured out a way for his troops to roar in harmony. Done right, it sounds like a ferocious mountain lion roar. He has used this tactic to scare others away from the forest, away from the old haunted barn, or into his traps. But, believe me, that's not the most dangerous part."

"So there's this magical army of warrior cats and a Ninja Coon? Do I have that right? I'm waiting to hear more because it's so amusing."

"It's not amusing at all. It's the truth," I say. "The most dangerous point is that this cat now has a rifle. I saw his troops bring it to him. With that rifle, this army of warrior cats can defeat anybody, even Animal Control."

"If that is all for your ridiculous tale—"

"That's not all, and it's not ridiculous. His name is Patches, and he plans to use the rifle to shoot Uncle Bill tonight in your barn. Then, he will take over the whole farm."

"Stop this nonsensical lying," Elmer says. "The barn animals will pronounce judgment on you for deception, Max's disappearance, and being an arrogant jerk. Our major concern is whoever is stealing eggs and fish. We can handle that problem on our own. We won't enter the forest, anyways. It's only natural that a mountain lion should have his domain in the forest."

My fur stands on edge when Elmer mentions that I will be under judgment from the farm animals. Elmer doesn't understand that he can't relax on the farm and do nothing. Whether they like it or not, Patches and his troops will attack the farm tonight.

"Enter the barn to meet your accusers," Elmer says, "but I warn you. Don't try any of your tricks, or a large cow or horse will trample you."

Before we enter the barn, a sobbing sound turns Elmer and I towards the forest. The middle boy child comes out of the woods with his father. I already know that the middle boy child has a black eye, and probably a bloody nose, too.

"I'm telling the truth!" the middle boy child says, raising his voice. "There were giant house cats in that forest, and they took the rifle! It wasn't me! It wasn't me! It was giant cats!"

"Let's get Mom or Aunt Susie to patch you up. Once you get your wits about yourself, you'll remember what really happened," the big man person says.

"See?" I say to Elmer. "The boy child knows the truth. He knows those cats have the rifle. Those cats are the same ones who took Alfie. Alfie lost his life to them."

***

"*Alfie?*" Elmer gasps.

"You see?!" I say to Elmer. "There's proof. Just like I said. Patches' troops stole the rifle, and the middle boy child witnessed it. The other teenage boys think he stole their rifle, and that's why they gave him a black eye."

"I can't trust you. You're up to something," Elmer says.

"Trust me for one more night," I tell Elmer, "and then you will see that I'm telling the truth. We will save Uncle Bill's life, his farm, and all of you."

"This is all ridiculous," Elmer says.

"You heard the middle boy child," I say. "It fits exactly with what I told you. If you don't trust me, and I'm right, then think of what will happen. With Patches in charge, the farm lost, and Uncle Bill shot, you would be glad to have a coyote ruling over you. It's worse than that. Patches doesn't just want to kill Uncle Bill; he wants to go on and take over the whole world! Tonight, you will see that I am telling the truth. You have nothing to lose if you trust me based on the witness of that middle boy child."

"You have a point," Elmer concedes. He wiggles his nose as he ponders the situation. I ready myself to run away if he refuses. Of course, I don't know where I would run to.

"I will trust you for one night," Elmer says as he looks me in the eyes. He leans in, and says, "But on one condition."

"What would that be?"

"You must give a full confession of all your lies, and you must give a full apology to all the farm animals."

It's a good thing my imaginary Chief adviser gave me this very same advice. Somehow, I knew deep down this would have to happen.

Elmer adds, "And don't you dare give one of those fake apologies where you say something like, 'I am sorry if I offended you.' You need to give a real apology, like, 'This is how I lied to you, and I was wrong. Please forgive me.'"

"But what about—?"

"Don't you dare try to justify why you told those lies. Clearly state what you did wrong, apologize, and then ask for their forgiveness. Got it?"

"I agree."

I follow Elmer into the barn, and the farm animals rustle back into their pens. They must have been gathered at the door, straining to hear our discussion. I imagine Chief nearby in his pen, watching and cheering me on.

The farm animals murmur angrily amongst themselves.

"She lies!" Wyatt the rat calls out. A rumbling of agreement rises from the other farm animals.

"Distinguished animals of Uncle Bill's barn," Elmer says to the farm animals, "I respectfully request that you listen to what Princess has to say. Princess first wishes to apologize. Then, she will tell us about the larger issues at stake. I have decided that we will trust her for just this one night. If she is telling the truth, we can't afford not to do so." Elmer steps aside and motions for me to stand in the center of the barn. "The floor is yours, Princess."

I move to the center of the barn, and I look around. Elmer stands off to the side. Benny the wiener dog stands on the opposite side. Wyatt the pretender millionaire rat rests on the edge of the hayloft. Ned the interviewing horse is in his pen, and Gus and Betsy, the art critic sheep, are in an adjacent pen. David and Lisa, the vegan goats, are in their pens. Daisy stands directly in front of me, chewing on her cud.

"I beg your attention, distinguished animals of Uncle Bill's barn," I say with all the authority I can muster. A chorus of boos and hisses flies back at me. "When I first arrived, I came as a visitor from a distant land. I did not know what I would find, but I discovered a new world. A new world full of possibilities, but also full of flaws. I recognized that you needed a savior. You needed a more civilized and cultured vision of the world."

I glance over to Elmer, and he glares at me. The boos and hisses are louder now.

"She continues to lie," Gus the sheep yells.

I need to get to the point and come clean.

"I confess," I say, "to you first of all that I wanted to rule the farm after Alfie left. You have to admit, things were falling apart. I mean, think about it. Benny the wiener dog is so small, he can't scare anybody away. And Wyatt the rat, well, you are by no means a millionaire. You feast on table scraps. And you, Ned the interviewing horse, are meant to be ridden on by people, not listened to. And Pearl the poodle, I don't think I have to tell you how stuck up she is, convinced that she is a celebrity. She is her only fan! And Gus and Betsy, the art critic sheep, well, I cannot bear to hear you criticize another piece of art while you produce no art of your own. And David and Lisa, the vegan goats! Goats should eat anything and everything! Goats are nature's garbage disposal. Who are you to judge everybody else for what they choose to eat? And Daisy the investor cow? Really? Have you ever started or run a business? Or, do you simply dispense advice to anybody, even though you have no investment portfolio yourself?"

The animals are quiet, apparently shocked by my honesty. If Chief were here, he'd warn me that I need to get back on track. But I can't help myself. If I'm going to tell the truth and apologize, somebody needs to tell them the hard truth about their crazy dreams. I fear their astonishment will soon turn to anger.

"I know what happened to Alfie, and I will tell you. But I must begin my own confession. I originally planned to manipulate both Pearl and Benny. Benny is desperately in love with Pearl. He has a crush on her."

Benny blushes. It is difficult to hear the truth, especially in public.

"However, there's no chance Pearl will ever reciprocate that love. But I found a way. Pearl had lost her diamond-studded collar, and I knew that if I could find it and give Benny the credit, then perhaps Pearl would fall in love with Benny. I have found the collar, but she cares nothing for Benny."

Benny's eyes show a mix of anger and sadness. I'm not sure if he's holding back tears or angry barks. I do feel pity for him. If only he had known the truth sooner. Besides, she is so conceited that she would not be a good mate for him.

"I also lied," I continue, "about Max and Alfie at the farm next door. Let me tell you the whole truth. Afterward, there's a plan we must put into action. Otherwise, as Elmer has said, there will be dire and irreversible consequences.

"Let me remind you that things were falling apart when I arrived. This was evident by your secret invader. This secret invader stole eggs from the chicken coop, and you could do nothing about it. This secret invader stole fish from Uncle Bill. I discovered that it was this same secret invader who sabotaged Uncle Bill's tractor in an attempt to kill him.

"This invader was a giant and cunning raccoon. He was legendary. He was known as the Ninja Coon. But he was not the real threat. As you may have noticed, I refer to the Ninja Coon in the past tense. That is because the real threat is an army of warrior cats led by a cat named Patches. He used the Ninja Coon to chip away at the defenses of Uncle Bill's farm, but he has since dispensed with the Ninja Coon. I had wanted to capture the Ninja Coon to regain the stolen diamond-studded collar.

"However, I failed. Patches and his cat warriors were impatient and captured the Ninja Coon themselves. They gave me the diamond-studded collar that he had stolen from Pearl. Patches forced me to join his army. I had no choice. In order to prevent Patches from destroying Uncle Bill, his farm, and all of you, I had to temporarily work with Patches. My intent was to earn his trust and then cross him and defeat him.

"Max, however, refused to join Patches. Patches forced Max into his army, and he has since re-educated Max. Max is no longer the friendly, though foolish, partially grown cat you used to know. He has now become a hardened warrior, having forgotten his past life and those whom he knew. Max has not been at the farm next door with Alfie. Rather, he is now in Patches' army, and he is our enemy.

"The farm next door is simply abandoned. Alfie, I have learned, also refused to join Patches in the past, and Patches killed Alfie. That is the sad truth about Alfie. It is also the sad truth of what happened to Max, but Max survived the re-education; Alfie did not.

"That teenage boy who goes hunting with his friends was also after the Ninja Coon. His father hopes to buy the forestland and Uncle Bill's farm in order to develop it. So Patches has defeated the Ninja Coon, and his troops recently stole the teenage boy's rifle. He plans to use that rifle to shoot Uncle Bill tonight in this very barn. Then, he will take over the farm. After that, he plans to take over the whole world."

Everybody's mouth hangs open. I don't know if they are full of disbelief or surprise.

"This may be unbelievable to all of you," Elmer says, "but we do have evidence from the middle boy child that ferocious warrior cats have indeed stolen the rifle. We can't risk them using that against Uncle Bill."

"That's right," I say, "but with your help, we can carry out a plan that will defeat Patches, save Uncle Bill, his farm, and all of you."

CHAPTER 11

"Supposing we trust you," Ned the interviewing horse asks, "what is your plan?"

"We will all have to help for this plan to work," I say, "but I'm confident we can foil Patches' plan if we work together. First of all, somebody bring in the scarecrow from the field."

"We can do that," Gus volunteers.

"Put the scarecrow in the back of the barn," I say. "When Patches comes in with the rifle, he must think that the scarecrow is really Uncle Bill."

"We will not only bring the scarecrow in," Betsy the sheep says, "but we will also use our artistic sensibilities to make the scarecrow lifelike."

"Great idea," I say.

This may be the first time their obsession with art will benefit anybody.

"And so what if Patches does come in with his rifle and thinks the scarecrow is Uncle Bill?" Elmer asks.

"We should thank that old Ninja Coon, may he rest in peace," I say, "for crashing the tractor into the barn. I will drive the tractor through the hole in the side of the barn. With the attached mower, all I have to do is drive the tractor straight into the barn as fast as I can. It won't be pretty, but the tractor will either run over Patches and his troops, or it will mow them up." Most of the farm animals stare at me with disgusted alarm, except for Dave.

"If that mower decimates Patches and his troops," Dave the vegan goat says, "then that will be dozens fewer carnivores in this world." Lisa, his wife, beams with excitement.

"You really think that will work?" Benny asks. "Every plan is perfect until the real battle begins."

"I do have a backup," I say, "but it's not pretty either."

"What is your backup plan if you can't mow up Patches?" Ned the interviewing horse asks.

"Lock them in, and burn it down," I say.

I pull out the lighter I took from the teenage boys while they camped in the woods. I give it a flick, and a small flame appears. Everybody looks around the barn at all the hay bales. It wouldn't take much to send the whole barn up in flames.

"It would ruin Uncle Bill's barn, but it would destroy Patches, and it would save Uncle Bill."

"You can't burn the barn down while we're in it," Daisy the investor cow says.

"Of course not," I say. "Once the scarecrow is in place, everybody will sneak to the neighbor's abandoned barn and hide there."

"This is a delicate operation," Ned the interviewing horse says. "How do you suppose all of us can sneak to the other barn without being noticed by Patches, Uncle Bill, or that nosy Pearl?"

"Uncle Bill is going fishing again today," I say. "That means he's good for nothing for the whole day. Patches will be resting and preparing for the attack tonight. If he isn't, he won't care if everybody goes to a different barn. All he cares is that I get Uncle Bill into the barn tonight so that he can shoot Uncle Bill with the rifle."

"Can I be in charge of distracting Pearl?" Benny asks.

"Okay," I say. "We will work together to distract Pearl so she doesn't sound the alarm for Aunt Susie that all of her farm animals are walking away."

"What a sorry lot we will look, exiled from our own barn," Gus the sheep says.

"It's no joking matter," I say. "If Pearl sounds the alarm, the plan will be ruined. Aunt Susie would get Uncle Bill. He would examine the barn to discover why you were all leaving. He would be precisely where Patches wants him."

***

My plan begins well. Uncle Bill goes fishing with the children and my big man person for the morning. They plan to drive into town and go shopping after lunch. Aunt Susie says she wants to clean the house in the morning, but she's not interested in going shopping after lunch. This is unfortunate, but it's not an insurmountable problem. We will have to figure out how to prevent Pearl from alerting Aunt Susie when the farm animals leave.

By midmorning, Gus and Betsy the sheep have hauled in the scarecrow, and they're busy making it look exactly like Uncle Bill.

"This is easy because the scarecrow is made from Uncle Bill's old clothes," Gus says.

"Yes, but I have never fancied myself an artist of such mixed media," Betsy says.

"It doesn't have to be perfect," I say. "It only has to be good enough to fool Patches for a short time. Then, I will start the tractor, drive in, and mow up all those bad cats."

I go to talk with Benny. He can't like the fact that even though Pearl thinks he recovered her diamond-studded collar, Pearl is not in love with him.

"I need to tell you more about Pearl," I say. "Aunt Susie bought her a newer and better collar. Her old diamond-studded collar is meaningless to her. Therefore, you are meaningless to her."

"I… I can't believe it," Benny says.

"It's the truth," I say. "But there is good news hidden in this difficult truth."

I feel that maybe Chief himself is dispensing wisdom through me to Benny.

"These circumstances revealed Pearl's true character. If she were to love you now, how would you consistently perform heroic acts to re-earn her love? She's not the girl you have been dreaming of. She would be a cruel master, and you would constantly try to re-earn her love as her affections shift from one shiny object to the next."

"I need to talk to her myself," Benny says. "If what you're saying is true, I need to hear it myself."

"We can go to Pearl this afternoon," I say to Benny. "Once Uncle Bill goes into town shopping and leaves Aunt Susie with Pearl at home, we can find a way inside to talk with Pearl. Don't get your hopes up, though."

Benny purses his lips and stares ahead. I think he's trying to hold back tears.

"Trust me," I say. "Even though it might be hard right now, Pearl isn't right for you. Perhaps there is somebody else out there who is."

"Who?" Benny asks. He looks directly at me to challenge me. "There are just a bunch of farm animals here."

"You're right," I say, "and you need to do your job as a true guard dog and serve your master, Uncle Bill. The way to do that is to help me this afternoon. Nobody else can be in the barn when Patches shows up this evening. But if Pearl spots a train of farm animals walking out of Uncle Bill's barn this afternoon, she will alert Aunt Susie. For all of our friends' sake, and for Uncle Bill's sake, we need to make sure that doesn't happen."

Benny sets his jaw, looks me in the eyes, and says, "You're right. I'll protect the farm animals, and I will faithfully serve my master."

"If we fail this afternoon, we have no hope of defeating Patches."

***

I wait until my people drive away with Uncle Bill to go shopping before I tell Benny it's time to talk with Pearl. We have to keep her distracted long enough so that she doesn't yap her head off when she sees an exodus of farm animals.

"I'll go inside and see what it's like," I say. "If we're lucky, Aunt Susie will be busy, and we can both walk right into Pearl's room and have a talk with her."

"I'll stand guard," Benny says dutifully as he sits down next to the doggy door.

I pass through the doggy door, and I hop up onto the rafters that run under the cathedral ceiling. I don't go far before discovering Aunt Susie's location. Aunt Susie reclines on the couch in front of the television, snoring. A very popular television show is on. Even I recognize it. The lady on television holds an insane amount of influence over people. Perhaps I need my own TV show. Pearl lies on the floor between Aunt Susie and the TV. It will be tricky to get Pearl away without waking Aunt Susie.

Once I'm back outside, I tell Benny the plan.

"You go to the kitchen. You'll see it. I'll wake Pearl up and lead her into the kitchen to talk with us. We have to be quiet because Aunt Susie is asleep in the living room watching TV. Got it?"

"Got it."

Benny follows me into the house. I nod towards the kitchen, and Benny softly walks there, glancing over at Pearl. I hop onto the rafters and make my way directly above Aunt Susie and Pearl.

"Pssst," I whisper to Pearl. Aunt Susie continues snoring.

If this snoring won't wake her, how can I wake her?

"Pssst. Pearl," I say as loudly as I dare. Aunt Susie continues snoring, and Pearl doesn't notice. I will have to do this the hard way. I climb down and slink my way under the couch that Aunt Susie is sleeping on. Once I'm confident she is still deep in sleep, I crawl over to Pearl and tap her.

"Pearl, it's me, Princess."

Pearl emits a yawn, rolls over, and says, "I don't feel like a photo shoot today..."

I don't know who Pearl thinks she is, but even for a dog, she is incomprehensible. I give her two sharp pokes, and then I clasp my paw over her mouth so that she doesn't make a noise.

Her eyes are wide open as she looks at me, and I have to tell her, "Don't worry, it's just me. Be quiet."

Her eyes say: "What are you doing?"

I remove my paw from her mouth to answer, but before I do, she says, "I can't believe I fell asleep during the show." Disappointment hangs in Pearl's voice.

"I'm sure it will be on again later," I reassure her. "Come to the kitchen. We need to talk."

Pearl follows me into the kitchen with a yawn.

She doesn't acknowledge Benny. Instead, she hops up onto a chair in the breakfast nook and curls up.

"What did you want to talk about?" Pearl asks. "I'm not sure I will be able to squeeze it into my schedule."

Benny and I move under the table of the breakfast nook. We can see out through the sliding glass doors. Pearl, laying on her chair, is the only thing obstructing our view into the yard. Thankfully, Pearl faces away from the sliding glass door.

Just as I am about to address Pearl, Elmer gallantly begins to lead the farm animals out of the barn.

He is finally getting his chance to be a shepherd.

I need to hold Pearl's attention long enough that she doesn't turn around.

"Pearl," I begin, "I want to personally introduce you to Benny. He is a brave and loyal dog, and he saved your diamond-studded collar at great cost."

"I have no interest in... whoever..." Pearl says with a roll of her eyes. "Am I forgetting, or did we already talk about this?"

"We did talk about this," I say, stalling for time, "but I don't think I explained to you exactly how wonderful and heroic Benny is. You see, he rescued the diamond-studded collar from a beast of the forest. Armed men had been hunting this beast for years without success. Elite hunting dogs had been hunting down this beast for years, and failed. But Benny, because of his love for you, tracked down this beast, slayed it, and took from it what rightfully belongs to you. He risked his life just so you could have your diamond-studded collar."

I see that Ned the interviewing horse is well on his way out of the barn, and behind him are David and Lisa, the vegan goats. Gus and Betsy come next, and they are deep in conversation. They are no doubt discussing the finer points of some long-dead French Impressionist painter.

Can't they go faster?

I haven't seen Daisy leave the barn yet.

"Benny is a fool for risking his life for such a silly thing," Pearl says.

"Are you sure you shouldn't reconsider?" I persist, even though I know the answer.

I need more time. All of the animals are not out of the barn yet.

"Of course I'm certain," Pearl says. "I could never fall in love with the wiener dog." That insult hurts even me, and I look over to see a dejected Benny. But Benny is smart enough to see we need to buy more time.

Finally, Daisy the investor cow meanders out of the barn, and Elmer is at her heels, prodding her along. Many of the other farm animals are already out of view.

Come on Daisy, move it.

Just when I think Benny and I can leave, Gus—or maybe it's Betsy—rushes back into the barn.

What could be the problem? That's the wrong way!

"A celebrity of your status needs a bodyguard," I say, desperate to hold Pearl's attention. "Benny is the ideal bodyguard. He is a formidable force, as he demonstrated by defeating the beast in the forest. I don't think I need to mention how devoted he is to you."

"Interesting idea," Pearl says. "I do need a bodyguard. I will have to think about it."

Just in time, the last sheep departs the barn, heading in the correct direction. Elmer herds him along quickly, but then I see Elmer go back into the barn.

Do these animals have no sense of urgency?

Seconds later, Elmer rushes out of the barn. Once he's out of view, I know Benny and I have done our job.

"Give that some thought then," I tell Pearl, "and maybe we can talk more about it in a few days. Like I said, a celebrity of your stature deserves at least one bodyguard."

Pearl doesn't respond. She rotates so that she faces out the window. She's now in the sun.

Just in time.

I nod for Benny to follow me, and we leave the house for the barn.

"I'll make sure the scarecrow is exactly as it should be," I say, "but you need to go to the other barn."

"I've got something to say, Princes," Benny says.

I stop and turn around to look at him.

"Thank you for telling me the truth about Pearl," Benny says. "It hurts, but sometimes the truth does hurt."

Not as much as lies hurt.

We part ways, but after a quick examination of the scarecrow in the barn, which looks lifelike to me, I catch up to Benny.

We don't talk as we impatiently trot to the abandoned barn to meet all the other farm animals. It's an eerie feeling. We pass the far cow pasture, go through some light woods, and then we come to the barn. I don't know how long it has been empty, but now it's full of Uncle Bill's animals.

When we enter the barn, everybody quiets down, and they look at me as if I have new orders to give. I don't know what to say, but I'm thankful that everybody is safe in this barn.

"I'll head back to Uncle Bill's barn to make sure everything is ready," I say. "You all stay put here. Good work. All of you."

I take a few steps out of the barn, but then I turn back.

"On second thought," I say after I reenter, "I will stay here with all of you until I have to go back to Uncle Bill's barn."

I do just that. I sit around in the barn and try to have fun with the animals. It feels good to be with them, but I think we're all in a state of denial about what's going to happen tonight.

When it starts to get dark, I say goodbye and head back to Uncle Bill's farm to make sure everything is ready. Dark clouds gather, and I wonder if I will encounter yet another thunderstorm at Uncle Bill's farm.

CHAPTER 12

When I arrive at Uncle Bill's barn, I can't imagine what will take place here tonight. It is a serene country setting. The manicured green grass nearby, prairie grass on the side, a forest in the distance, and wide-open areas, all combine to make this a postcard-perfect farm.

But Uncle Bill doesn't know what evil waits in the forest. I look in that direction, and dark rain clouds have moved slightly closer. A distant thunder faintly rumbles, but I doubt we will get any rain tonight.

After I do a few circles around the tractor to make sure it is in the right spot—and it is—I hop up to make sure the keys are still in the ignition. That's one thing I've learned about the country. People just leave the keys in.

All I will have to do is press this *button, push down on* this, *push down on this, pull* that *lever, and I will send the tractor hurtling through the hay bales and into the barn with the mower running.*

That should be the end of Patches. In case that doesn't work, I go inside the barn to prepare the backup plan.

I look for the lighter I stole from the teenage boys, but it's not where I left it.

My backup plan can't work if I don't have a lighter to start the fire!

I spread hay all around the perimeter of the barn as I search for the lighter. I push some piles of hay near the larger posts. I grab a small gas can from the tractor, and I sprinkle gas around the barn. When I strike the lighter, flames will encircle the whole barn and engulf Patches in an inferno.

I hope rain doesn't put the fire out, I think as I notice the clouds creep closer.

I inspect the scarecrow inside, and I am proud of Gus and Betsy's art. If I didn't know any better, I would think Uncle Bill is standing in the back corner of this barn.

I get an idea, just in case.

Gas sloshes inside the gas can as I haul it over and pour extra gasoline on the scarecrow. If Patches attacks the scarecrow, I want to make sure the scarecrow burns up really good.

I climb up into the hayloft, searching for the lighter and any openings that would allow Patches to escape. I spot Wyatt's home. Something catches my eye, and so I move closer. It's a giant magazine. *Cigar Spectator* is scrawled across the top.

I shake my head as I go to inspect Gus and Betsy's pen below. I see a good-sized hole in the slats that form the wall. I block it with nearby wood so that Patches would not be able to escape.

I discover that Gus and Betsy, like Wyatt, have their own literature. It is a brochure from the *Institute of Art*. It's well worn. I have to admit, I would like to see them get the opportunity to gaze at a true masterpiece with their own eyes.

David and Lisa's pen doesn't allow any potential escape routes for Patches. Instead of books or magazines, partial stems of kale litter the pen.

Just because goats eat kale doesn't mean kale is edible.

Ned's pen reveals nothing, but I find an old copy of an investing newspaper in Daisy the investing cow's pen. Elmer left behind one of his books: *How to Win People and Influence Friends*. Elmer does have a knack for leadership, but I prefer the book, *The Prince*. Just one last place to check: the main door into the barn.

I grab a nearby rope and tie it to the door handle. Then I go outside to test it. If I light the barn on fire, all I have to do is run out before Patches realizes what is happening. Then I pull this rope, and the barn door will slam shut, locking Patches inside the burning barn.

But I still haven't found the lighter!

I wonder if the farm animals got the magazines, brochures, and books from Alfie. I see now that Alfie did exercise influence over his domain. But—

Vroom! Vroom, Vrrroooom!

The tractor roars to life. I dash over, and I see Uncle

Bill, who has apparently come back from shopping, seated in the driver's seat. I freeze, not knowing what to do. Uncle Bill backs the tractor up and drives it towards the far cow pasture. When Uncle Bill is nearly out of sight, I'm still sitting with my mouth gaping open. A bird could have flown in and built a nest.

I can't use the tractor to save Uncle Bill's life if he drives it away!

I need to find out where the tractor is going. I run towards the cow pasture, and when I get there, I find that Uncle Bill has parked it under a lean-to near the cow pasture. Uncle Bill stops the tractor, gives it a pat and says, "Herbie will be able to fix you up right here."

He couldn't wait until tomorrow?

I mope back towards Uncle Bill's barn. Burning down the barn is the only plan I have left—if I can find the lighter. I don't look forward to burning down Uncle Bill's barn, but that may be the only option.

Just as I reach the barn to search for the lighter, I realize:

I'll bet Wyatt the rat took the lighter for a cigar.

But then I hear barking from two different directions. I turn and see Dan running out of the woods towards me. I turn in the other direction, back towards the cow pasture, and I see Benny running towards me.

They reach me at the same time, and they're both frantically out of breath. They can hardly get out what they're trying to say.

They say, nearly in unison, "Patches is going to the other barn over there!"

After they both yell this out, they give each other a confused look, and then Benny smiles slightly as Dan looks away.

I hurry over to the neighbor's barn so that I get there before Patches does. I don't want to know what he has planned for those unsuspecting farm animals.

***

The prairie grass brushes against me as I nearly fly through it. I pass through the light woods, barely aware of Benny and Dan following me. Patches must have known I moved the farms animals, and that it signaled my betrayal. I was wrong to think he wouldn't care. How can I get Patches back to Uncle Bill's barn so that I can burn it down with him inside of it? As I enter the clearing of the neighboring barn, I notice the gathering storm clouds. A thunderstorm appears likely.

I pray to the feline gods that Wyatt has the lighter.

As I approach the barn, I smell the expected farm animals, but the stench of feral cats overpowers my feline senses. Patches has beaten me here. Benny and Dan smell it before I do, and they whimper as we draw near to the barn.

I look to Benny and say, "If you want to be a guard dog, you have to be willing to face some scary bad guys."

Benny narrows his eyes, sets his jaw towards the barn, and forces one foot in front of another as he follows me to the barn.

"Dan, thank you for the warning, but this isn't your fight. Go back to your master."

"Those disgusting cats stole my master's rifle, and they have been a nuisance in the forest. I will be glad to face them."

I'm only inches away from entering the barn, and I feel a sense of pride that Benny is brave enough to face Patches for the sake of the farm animals. I'm also slightly comforted by the fact that I have a hunting hound, although not yet fully grown, coming with me.

I walk into the barn, but it's dark, just like Patches' old haunted barn was. There's only a slight ruffling of the farm animals, who must be in pens or stalls. Pairs of cat eyes encircle me on the perimeter of the barn.

A dim ray of moonlight shines through a crack in the roof and falls onto the center of the barn floor.

Patches steps into the ray of moonlight.

"My troops have all of your farm friends trapped," Patches says. "I never trusted you. I knew you were accustomed to pretending to be in charge at your house with your pathetic people. You are overconfident because you defeated Snarl.

"Trainee 44 confirmed this truth to me. You didn't defeat Snarl. You got lucky; you discovered the danger of the broken garage door on accident. Once my spies spotted all the farm animals making their way to this abandoned barn, I knew for certain you had betrayed me.

You were moving them to supposed safety."

There is no point in continuing my lie. I had hoped that I would be able to cross Patches at a critical point and defeat him, but he learned too soon that I was never loyal to him.

"Not only is your fame as the slayer of Snarl illegitimate, but look at you now. You rely on dogs. That is nearly as foolish as caring about people."

"Let the farm animals go," I say. "They have no business with you. There's no reason to have innocent blood on your paws. Let them go."

"You don't understand," Patches says, taking a step towards me with a low growl rising in his chest. "There are no innocents. Everybody is either for me or against me. Everybody not for me is against me, and therefore not innocent."

Before I can respond, Patches leaps out of the moonlight, and I hear what sounds like ripping fabric accompanied by gnashing teeth, and then a thud. I hear a weak whimper from Benny, who has been attacked and thrown against the barn wall by Patches. Dan lets out a sharp bark and growls while pouncing for Patches. Patches is more elusive than the dot from a laser pointer, and Dan misses. Patches hops onto Dan's back, bites the scruff of his neck and claws furiously. Dan twists around, yelping and screaming. Patches hops off and gives him a kick with his two hind legs. Dan tumbles into the perimeter of Patches' troops. They restrain both Benny and Dan.

"Enough!" Patches yells. "Hold those mongrel mutts still while I have some fun with Princess. We will deal with them later."

Before I realize what is happening, Patches lunges at me and bowls me over, knocking the wind out of me. At once he's on top of me and bats me from side to side with a paw. I try to lash out, but he simply bats me back in the other direction with his other front paw. He does this one or two more times before I'm able to get one swipe in at his nose.

He backs away playfully and lunges with his jaws open. His fangs dig in to my neck. I try to raise up my rear claws to slash at him, but he does the same with his more powerful legs. There is no way I can counter this, and it is only a matter of time before things will go black for me. Instead, Patches releases his grip and backs away.

He's done playing with me.

"This is far too easy," Patches boasts to his troops. "I would find it more entertaining if you fought somebody else. Let me think. I know. I will allow your old apprentice, Trainee 44, to finish you off. You will discover that I have molded him into a real cat during his brief tutelage."

Patches looks behind him and gives a slight nod. A few seconds later, Max steps into the moonlight. As I noticed before at the old oak tree, he is still mostly orange. But now his white paws have dried blood on them, and the white spot on his back is mostly pulled out. He has more scratches and burns. Max appears even fiercer than he did at the old oak tree.

A week ago, defeating Max in a fight would have been easy. But now I'm sure that even if I were to defeat Max with difficulty, Patches would finish me off.

***

Trainee 44 is Max, but I can scarcely believe it. I remember him less than a year ago gingerly approaching me as I slept in my favorite sunbeam. I recall his countless distractions by butterflies, dandelions, roly-polies, and any shiny object. That Max no longer exists.

Did Patches force him to drink strange toilet water?

I need to snap Max out of whatever Patches has done to him.

Max has only been with Patches for a few days, and yet the transformation is amazing.

He leaps at me with never before possessed agility and ferocity. Max launches at me a second and a third time, but I evade each in turn.

"Max," I say, "you don't want to do this. It's me, Princess."

"I know exactly who you are," Max says just before another lunge. I barely dodge him, but one of his claws catches my hind leg that was injured during my duel with Snarl. I thought I had recovered from the injury, but a sharp pain shoots up my leg and into my back.

Does Max remember my old injury?

Nobody else would know about this injury.

"Get away! You can do it!" Elmer shouts.

"You savage, Patches. Make this stop!" David the vegan goat yells. "Such barbarism!"

"Max! It's us!" Betsy the art critic sheep calls out. "It's us and Princess!"

But Max presses on, continually lunging after me, trying to pin me down so that he can bite and slash me.

My energy fades. Max wears me down.

I dodge his next attack by a whisker, but Max lunges again, and he's on top of me.

I shield my neck from his fangs, but he clamps down on my leg instead.

Pain shoots throughout my body.

I twist to get away, but I'm unable to escape his grasp. His fangs search for soft flesh to inflict maximum damage.

"If you are really on my side," I whisper, "and you will betray Patches, then give me a sign."

Max's assault continues, seeking a vulnerable spot for his fangs.

"Give me three quick scratches with your hind claws if you are really against Patches," I whisper. I hope Max is putting on a charade so that he can turn against Patches at a key moment as I originally hoped to do.

Instead of three quick scratches, he goes into a fury. He scratches repeatedly with both hind feet. The pain is unbearable, and my vision begins to go black.

A deep survival instinct must kick in, because I twist around with all my remaining strength. I escape for a second.

"Get back here," Max commands.

He lunges at me. I dodge once, but Max lunges again. He sinks his fangs into the scruff of the back of my neck, and my body goes limp. He's using the attack I taught him for coyotes as a kitten: The Guillotine. I will not survive the attack.

"Halt!" Patches calls out.

There is silence and stillness in the barn.

"Take her over there," Patches commands his troops. Max gets off of me, and Patches' troops pull me over to a hay bale against the wall.

The hay bale reeks, and the odor shocks me back to consciousness. I recognize the odor. It's the same fuel I spread in Uncle Bill's barn.

"Come over here, Max," Patches says, "and put this rifle to good use. Then, your training will be complete."

Patches' troops hold me in place in front of the hay bale. Max sits next to Patches behind the rifle. The rifle points at me.

The farm animals moo, bleat, and screech to protest my impending execution.

My life, and my reign as empress, will end at the hand of Max. I refuse to beg. I shut my eyes for the end.

Bang!

Bang!

***

If this is heaven, I'm honestly a little disappointed.

Two dead cats lie on either side of me.

This isn't cat heaven.

Max shot Patches' troops instead of me.

Everything happens at once in chaos.

The animal pens open to allow the farm animals out. Benny and Dan must have broken away to undo the latches.

Patches' troops pounce on Max, and Patches wrestles the rifle away. He slinks up to the hayloft, pulling the rifle with him.

Did Max try to turn the rifle on Patches?

I slouch to the ground, exhausted and wounded; Patches' troops leave me for dead. The barn is in an uproar, but I witness it through a haze from my injuries.

Ned the horse and Daisy the cow use their size in the fight. Cats leap and claw at them, but they buck around the barn like broncos at the rodeo. When their hind leg strikes a cat, it flies and smacks into the barn wall.

Elmer shepherds the smaller animals out of the barn. Before David the vegan goat leaves, he coughs a few times, and he regurgitates something for Elmer.

It's my lighter!

David the vegan goat ate *my lighter to hide it from Patches and sneak it in here?*

"Ned! Daisy!" Elmer yells. "It's time to get out of here!"

Elmer flicks a flame to life from the freshly vomited lighter. Immediately, a ring of fire encircles the barn. That's why the hay bale smelled like fuel. Elmer had planned ahead to take action once he knew Patches was coming.

Need to get the tractor.

Warrior cats swarm Ned, Daisy, and Max as I sneak out of the barn.

Adrenaline masks the pain as I shuffle on three legs towards the tractor.

I catch up to the confused and fleeing herd of farm animals.

Pain begins to pulse in my leg just as I reach the tractor. The farm animals continue towards Uncle Bill's barn. I hop up onto the tractor and get ready to start it, and Daisy and Ned run past.

Wyatt is about to escape from the barn, but a cat pounces on him. Elmer bowls the cat over with his snout, and Wyatt escapes, but several cats drag Elmer back into the fire.

Uncle Bill and my big man person come running from Uncle Bill's house. They must have noticed the fire. They run past me and the tractor, but the heat stops them before they get too close to the barn.

I spot Patches hauling the rifle behind him towards Uncle Bill and my big man person. They won't notice Patches, and they certainly won't expect Patches to shoot them.

It's time to get this tractor started and put the mower into action. I press the button and pull the levers, praying to the feline gods that this tractor will run long and far enough to mow Patches over.

The tractor roars to life.

Thank the feline gods.

I aim the steering wheel at Patches, engage the drive, put the pedal to the metal, and head directly for Patches. The tractor jostles angrily as we go over bumps without concern for my comfort. I keep the pedal pressed down to go as fast as possible. Just as I reach Uncle Bill and my big man person, they see me coming and dive out of the way, no doubt astonished by the speeding tractor.

I have another problem. I can't press the pedal and turn the steering wheel at the same time. Out here in the wide open, Patches will dodge the tractor and the mower's spinning blades with ease. I see something even worse as I careen towards Patches.

Patches aims the rifle at Uncle Bill. I imagine him squinting through the sights to aim. I won't reach him in time before he shoots Uncle Bill.

Thud.

The tractor hits a bump that sends us off course. A moment later, we crash into a fencepost, and I fly out of the tractor.

I have no remaining plan.

The tractor is useless, and Elmer already burnt down one barn.

My plan has failed. Patches survives, and the rifle aims at Uncle Bill.

Boom!

The shot of the rifle—or was it thunder?—jolts my crippled body.

Boom!

There was no flash from the rifle. There's no lightning from the clouds.

The tractor backfired.

It's not thunder, but it has the same effect as thunder.

The herd of cows begins to rumble, and I know a stampede is brewing.

Boom!

Another backfire from the old tractor.

What a blessed old piece of junk.

The last backfire sends the cows into a stampede. It's exactly what I need. The cows stampede directly towards Patches and his remaining troops. Patches can't ignore the tidal wave of cows. He yells to his troops, and they flee for safety towards the forest.

The feline gods must be with me.

The herd of cows veer to chase Patches and his troops into the forest.

***

The stampeding cattle trample many of Patches' troops. This is the next best thing after a tractor with a mower.

"Hey! I'll give you a ride," Daisy the cow yells to me, snapping me out of my stupor. She's gasping heavily, but she intends to join the stampede. Ned gallops up a second later. Scratches and claw marks cover both of them, and their chests heave with exertion. There is a fight in their eyes I never saw at Uncle Bill's barn.

"We need to get that atrocious cat!" Ned the horse says. "This is a day for the ages!"

I hop onto Daisy's back, and with Ned at our side, we speed towards the forest.

There he is! I think to myself as I peek between Daisy's horns.

Patches limps as he hauls the rifle with him into the woods. The trees become more dense and dilute the stampede.

"Onward!" I urge. This could be our only chance to trample Patches, or at least to damage the rifle.

The thick forest canopy blocks moonlight and starlight. The burning barn behind us illuminates our path.

ROAR!

The fierce mountain lion roar rings out in the forest. Daisy and Ned rear up in fear. I'm tossed from Daisy's back.

I crash onto the ground, and pain radiates through my body. Ned and Daisy turn to flee out of the forest.

"Come back!" I yell from the ground. "It's not really a mountain lion! You can still…" I yell with all my strength, but I have little left. "It's a bluff! A lie!"

My voice is hoarse and full of gasps from injuries. Nobody could hear me unless they were right next to me. Daisy and Ned disappear from sight, assuming I am still on Daisy's back.

I look around the forest and assess my situation. The adrenaline fades, and the pain increases. I move to feel what's injured. Fierce scratches cover my back, but I can't see them. I only feel the pain. My previously injured leg is nearly useless, and now I only have three legs to use. One of my front legs has received a crushing bite.

Patches is about fifty feet away. He leans against a tree, doing something with the rifle. He's also injured. His patched fur is burnt from most of his body. He gasps heavy breaths. About six of his soldiers encircle him.

I try to drag myself behind a rock, but Patches' troops have already spotted me. I can feel their luminescent eyes lock on me.

I know they're coming for me. Patches laughs with gurgling breaths.

I hear movement and rustling from Patches, and I peek with one eye. The rifle is in position.

Click.

He is ready to shoot.

"Place her against the rock," Patches commands with a coarse voice. "I will finish her myself this time!"

Patches' troops are only feet away, and Patches lines up the rifle to aim at me. It will only be seconds until his troops hold me in place and Patches shoots me. There's no hope he will shoot his troops like Max did.

I will my body to stand and flee, but it is too broken and doesn't respond.

Just as the troops reach out to grab me, they suddenly leap away.

ROAR!

Another ferocious mountain lion roar rips through the air. I use all my strength to open my eyes. An immense yet agile beast passes over me in a blur.

A real mountain lion has leapt over me, and he swipes away Patches' troops with a gigantic paw.

The mountain lion turns and bores her yellow eyes into mine. A split second passes as the mountain lion decides what to do. She turns away from me and bounds directly for Patches.

The mountain lion leaps at Patches as the rifle fires. The bullet strikes a tree several feet from me. Patches missed.

Folks say the ghost of the mountain lion will never allow anybody else to rule the forest, I remember Uncle Bill saying around the fire at the weenie roast.

The mountain lion is upon Patches, tearing at him as a giant dog would a stuffed toy.

For now, I will live a few seconds longer. My body relaxes, I shut my eyes, and everything nearly goes black.

I don't know if it's seconds or minutes later, but I am being pulled on the ground. I drag along the dirt and leaves on the forest floor. I open one eye slightly, and I see a cat pulling me. He has burnt fur, but his body is orange with white feet and underbelly. Max is pulling me. He's pulling me from danger. The barn burns in the distance, but now it's an orange glow instead of tall yellow flames.

Heavy raindrops strike me, and then there's a flash of lightning and a thunderclap.

Everything goes black.

CHAPTER 13

I wake up, but I don't open my eyes. A warm sunbeam falls on me. I stretch slightly, but bandages restrict my movement. Dull aches creep through my body as my awareness returns.

Like a dream, I recall the vet bandaging me and giving me medicine. But was that last night, or when I was a kitten?

Where am I?

I succumb to exhaustion and fall back into a dreamlike state. I don't open my eyes. I move my ears slightly to bring in my surroundings, and I must be inside Uncle Bill's house. People move about: the big man person, the big woman person, the three children, and Uncle Bill and Aunt Susie.

"Max is so, so brave," the youngest girl child gushes. "He saved Princess."

"I'm surprised he bothered to save her," the big man person says, "after how mean she's been to him ever since we got him."

"Max is such a sweetie," the oldest girl child says.

"Is Max still sleeping?" the big man person calls into another room.

The middle boy child grunts. I've learned to interpret that as, "Yes."

"Max must be exhausted," the big woman person says. "He's sleeping a lot, even for a cat."

"If it hadn't been for Max pulling Princess out of the forest," Uncle Bill says, "the mountain lion would've gotten her for sure."

"But what happened to Max while he was missing?" the big man person asks. "It's like he went through feral cat boot camp plus bodybuilding. It's… bizarre."

"I think we will never know," Aunt Susie opines. "I'm glad that Pearl here is safe." I hear her scratching Pearl in her arms.

"The real mystery is who tried to steal away with my farm animals?" Uncle Bill says. "The vet says they'll all be better soon enough, except for Elmer. Poor guy, he lost his life in the fire. Who would've burned down the abandoned barn with the animals in it? I suppose it's the same person who sabotaged my tractor and then decided to take it for a joy ride last night. Never did see them."

"Come on," Aunt Susie says without hesitation. "We all know who is to blame."

"I suppose so," Uncle Bill says. "Some good is coming of it, too."

"Like what?" my big man person says.

"That developer who's been trying to take over my farm is no longer interested," Uncle Bill says.

"The police found a cigarette lighter," Aunt Susie says as she leans in to spill the juicy gossip. "It was the developer's teenage son's cigarette lighter. He's the one who started the fire. And the gunshots we heard that came from the barn just before it burned up? His rifle." She pauses for a second to let it sink in for everybody. "He sabotaged our tractor, and you could smell the fuel in our own barn too. He was going to burn our barn down." She allows another dramatic pause. Of course, I'm the one who poured fuel in Uncle Bill's barn to burn it down. "What a hooligan!"

"Calm down, Susie," Uncle Bill says. "We don't know that for sure."

"That's awful," the big man person says. But then he adds, "If it's true."

"The developer knows that the evidence points to his own son, and so he left before he got in real trouble," Aunt Susie says.

"So that's why he left that extra gift for Uncle Bill?" the big woman person says.

"He said his son wasn't responsible enough to own a dog," Uncle Bill says.

"And it looks like Dan and Benny are good friends already," the youngest girl person says.

Dan now belongs to Uncle Bill?

"You sure are right about that," Uncle Bill says. "They'll probably have puppies together."

Dan is a girl?

"I'm still curious about one thing, Uncle Bill," the big man person says. "I thought the mountain lion was just a story you told to keep the kids out of the woods."

"It was," Uncle Bill says, "for years. But then I started to hear a roar every now and then, but I'd never seen it. Not until last night, that is."

I'm safe and Max is safe. All the farm animals, except for Elmer who died to save Wyatt, are safe.

It's time for me to go back to sleep.

***

"Welcome back, Princess," Chief says. "How was your trip to the farm?" It doesn't take a detective to deduce from my injuries that I had some kind of adventure while at the farm. "What happened to you?"

Now that my family and I, along with Max, are back at our home, the farm seems like a different world.

"It was a good thing I was there, let me tell you," I say. "Who knows what would've happened if I hadn't shown up. It just goes to show that every place needs a cat in charge. Don't worry about the scratches. They will heal soon."

Chief raises his eyebrows after my comment. He must know that I received more than scratches.

"Did you make any new friends?" Chief asks.

"Not exactly," I say. But then, I realize that I did get to know some impressive animals. I can't help but share about them with Chief.

"On second thought, when I left the farm, I said farewell to some unique farm animals. First, there were Gus and Betsy, the art critic sheep. Kind of weird, I know, but they put their art knowledge to good use. We needed a scarecrow that looked like Uncle Bill, and they did exactly that. We ended up not needing it, but they still did a great job."

"Art critic sheep?" Chief asks.

"And don't forget Daisy and Ned," I say. "Daisy is a cow interested in finance, and Ned is a horse who dreams of being an interviewer. They set aside their craft when necessary, and they fought valiantly against an army of warrior cats."

"What kind of farm did you go to?" Chief asks.

"There's more," I say. "You can't forget David and Lisa, the vegan goats. Even though they keep a strict vegan diet, David swallowed a cigarette lighter to hide it from… Well, he regurgitated it when necessary to save everybody."

I decide not to mention Patches, who was nothing like Chief knew him.

"What in the world are you talking about?" Chief says. "Was everybody crazy at the farm?"

"Don't forget about Elmer, the sheepherder pig, and an excellent leader," I say. "He herded those animals away to safety, but he ended up paying the ultimate price himself. His leadership and sacrifice will never be forgotten."

Chief doesn't say anything to this. His mouth hangs open in disbelief.

"And of course it's a happy ending for Benny and Dan, *er, Danielle,* who are now in love," I say as I gaze off into the distance. Chief continues to stare, amazed.

I recount to Chief the whole story about the farm, but I never mention Patches by name. He does hear about all my lies, though.

"It sounds to me that lying got you in a whole heap of trouble," Chief says. There's too much amusement in his voice for my liking.

"And yet," I say, "Max pulled the biggest lie. He pretended to be a warrior cat until the very end, and then he saved me."

"Your story explains how Max was able to attack Todd when he came walking down the street and send him running," Chief says.

"We won't ever have to worry about Todd again."

"Yeah, but lies really mess things up," Chief says. "That teenage son of the developer, he wasn't guilty, but it sure ended up bad for him. He got blamed for everything. It worked out for you, though."

Chief has an interesting point. I guess I have about seven lives left. Otherwise, I can't figure out how I managed to survive all my lies, Patches' evil plan, and a real-life mountain lion.

That's not totally true. I survived because of Max. He saved my life.

Maybe Max should rule my domain. I can leave all the hard work to him while I bask in sunbeams without the worry of running an empire.

That seems like a plausible idea for only a few seconds.

Max is back to his old shenanigans. A butterfly leads him along the top of the woodpile until he stumbles off the edge. Several logs tumble down and narrowly miss him.

I had better continue ruling this domain.

Whirrrrr.

I can hear that can opener from anywhere.

A few minutes later, Max and I are inside my eating room, inhaling our canned cat food. And to think Patches thought that people are actually the ones in charge? Ridiculous. My people did all this work to serve me my food. Patches was wrong, and I am glad.

Cats rule the world.

After dinner, I want a quick nap in my favorite spot in my house. I head to the big people's bedroom, and I hop up onto the bed. I curl up into a ball at the head of the bed.

A minute or two later, I hear Max enter the room. He hops up onto the bed, and I feel the soft padding of his paws pressing into the mattress. He lays down and curls up at the foot of the bed.

I open my eyes and say, "Max, you can have the spot up here."

I get up, hop off the bed, and go outside for an evening stroll around my domain.

THE END.

Princess the Cat says:

"Join my newsletter. Be the first to know about my future adventures and get a free download: 'Top Five Animal Books to Read with Kids.'" A free prequel short story will also be available soon for subscribers.

You wouldn't want to disappoint Princess, would you?

www.bit.ly/FandFnewsletter

Author Notes:

If readers didn't detect any obvious homages to other children's books with animals, then I have some reading to suggest.

My children and I were captivated as we had read the classic, *Where the Red Fern Grows,* and it is the inspiration for the raccoon hunting. I even named the hunting hound Dan—or Danielle. Of course, when Princess steals the second letter of the big man person's note for Todd so Todd won't know to call when Princess and Max are missing is borrowed from *The Incredible Journey*. Lastly, Elmer the shepherd pig is a nod to *Babe,* and Ned is a reference to the classic Ed.

As with book one, the people don't really reflect how the real people in my life were. Princess and Max were real, and their personalities match what you have read, but I don't think they had such grand adventures! I did have a Great-Uncle Bill who was known as Uncle Bill, but he certainly didn't have a haunted barn in the woods near his house. And his wife wasn't Susie, and she didn't have a spoiled poodle. The name Susie is from Susie Dirkins of *Calvin and Hobbes* fame simply because I needed a female name.

I plan to have a prequel short story available exclusively for newsletter subscribers, so email me at john@flannelandflashlight.com, and I will add you to the list.

If you liked reading Princess' adventure, leave a review. It only takes a second, it helps me, and it could help somebody else discover Princess.

Until next time,
John Heaton
February, 2017

Princess the Cat Saves the Farm

Flannel and Flashlight Press
Cissna Park, IL

www.flannelandflashlight.com

***

First Print Edition

Made in the USA
Lexington, KY
29 June 2017